LETTERS IN BLUE

OUTBACK SKYE
BOOK 1

HEATHER REYBURN

Cover design: Patti Roberts (Paradox Book Cover Designs)

ISBN 978-0-6457440–8-8 Print Edition

Heather Reyburn

www.heatherreyburn.com

For my Skye friends, Millie, Sheila, Janette and Chris
Thank you

1

―――――

*I*sle of Skye, May 2024 – Ingrid

PEOPLE WATCHING WAS Ingrid Sloane's favourite pastime, and the stately man sitting at the bar of the Ardvasar Hotel drew her attention the moment she walked in. Shrouded in a tattered tweed jacket and emitting the faint smell of sheep and lanolin, it was his tie that intrigued her. She conceded that the sunny afternoon had ended with a cold, blasting gale that whipped the sea into a cauldron of froth and white-caps, so a coat was definitely a necessity. *Perhaps it's common practice here? Or perhaps it's this man's way of improving his dress code?* Whatever the reason, the bright blue fabric enhanced the twinkling sapphire of his eyes as he met Ingrid's gaze.

She slid onto the stool next to him, hesitating for a second as she considered the obvious generation gap between them. She held out her hand. 'Hi there. I'm Ingrid.'

He blinked, bushy eyebrows raised toward his dark, grey-peppered hair as he pushed the glass of chestnut liquid aside. After slowly reaching out, his work-worn paw clasped her fingers with surprising gentleness.

'Fergus MacRae.'

'Nice to meet you. Local?'

A tiny nod confirmed the answer before an awkward silence snagged her usually bubbly personality. Straightening her shoulders, she hesitated for only a moment. It was clear this man was not a talker. Or maybe he just took a while to open up. A challenge but not insurmountable.

From the doorway adjoining the bar and hotel kitchen, a middle-aged woman hurried toward them, wiping her hands on her apron. 'Sorry, folks. I thought Jack was taking care of you. Another drink, Fergus? Or are you ready for your tea?'

'Aye, Peggy.' He swallowed the last of his drink and placed his glass carefully on the counter. 'Jack's in the cellar changing the keg, so I'll wait a bit,' he said quietly. 'One more dram and I'll come through.' He cleared his throat, his eyes following Peggy's hand-wave toward his neighbour.

'Lovely.' She nodded. 'I see you've met our Australian visitor.' Peggy beamed at Ingrid while pouring Fergus another whisky. 'Come to the dining room whenever you're ready, Ingrid.'

'Thanks.' She looked at Fergus, burning to expand the conversation but acknowledging his obvious reticence. 'Please excuse me?'

The outside door opened, allowing a wintry blast to thrash Ingrid's bare legs as she followed Peggy through to the dining room, her step slowing to match the manager's. There was something about the Scotsman in the bar that provoked her interest. Not only his clothing, but the sad hint of acceptance encircling him—something that spoke of privacy and a touch of loneliness. She got that.

Guided to a small table by the smiling wait staff, Ingrid noted the others in the room—an older couple showing enormous interest in their meals but little for each other, a group of four young hikers, their faces flushed and seemingly oblivious to anyone around them, and a teenager in the opposite corner, her pretty face engrossed in her phone.

'I will bring the menu.' Heavily accented tones drew Ingrid's curiosity to the young woman in front of her. Dressed in a dark apron and with a notepad and pen in her hand, the waitress seemed another interesting visitor.

'Are you on a working holiday?' Ingrid asked.

'Yes.' The girl smiled, her brown plait swinging over one shoulder. 'I am from Germany and have the whole summer season here. I will go home in October. Lots of hiking to do between now and then,' she finished.

Ingrid returned her smile. 'I am from Australia and unfortunately my holiday is almost over. I would love to spend more time exploring these beautiful isles, but I guess I'll have to come back another time.' She pulled a face as the girl smiled and walked away, surprised how disappointed she felt voicing the very real fact. In less than a week, she would be in her uniform, scurrying up and down corridors tending to the very ill and the not-so-much. And, after each shift, every free moment would be spent helping her parents. She loved them dearly—but the next few months would be light years away from a holiday.

She made her meal choice then lay the menu on the table and waited until the girl returned.

'I'm Anna,' the waitress said.

Ingrid brightened as they discussed the places Anna had enjoyed most since arriving on Skye. When Anna returned to the kitchen, Ingrid felt suddenly bereft. Empty. Should she email her supervisor and extend her holiday? There was so much more here she wanted to explore—not only the land but the people too.

As the responsibilities of home crashed around her, she sank into her chair at the same time that Fergus entered the dining room.

HE SAT at the table next to hers and shot her a shy smile. 'I recommend the venison pie. No one does them better than Peggy.'

She had chosen the chicken but nodded. 'I'll try that tomorrow night.'

'Here for a while?'

'Three more days. Not enough to see everything I want to but ...' She shrugged. 'My time is limited due to other commitments.'

'Och well. If the weather clears and you can see beyond your toes tomorrow, you can't beat a stroll up the hills. The view over the Sound still takes my breath away—and I was born here.'

'You've been here all your life?'

'Aye. Mostly. This is my home.'

She smiled, hoping he would invite her to join him at his table so they could continue the conversation. But he didn't and their meals arrived, so she laid her serviette on her lap and began to eat.

IN THE ROOM above the hotel bar, Ingrid rose early, pulled the curtain to one side, and grinned. The skies were clear. Although from the coat almost engulfing the woman striding along the road below, it appeared to be cold. She dressed quickly, tied her long blonde hair in a ponytail, swiped a blob of sunscreen over her lightly tanned nose and cheeks, and trotted down the stairs to the dining room, determined to make the most of every minute she had left on this beautiful isle.

After a quick breakfast and chat with Peggy, she headed outside and stood on the roadside, breathing in the fresh sea air. Seagulls swirled above her, their raucous calls adding to the chug of a boat and the bleat of nearby sheep—noises betraying a rural seaside village. She struck out on the narrowing road that led through the village and up the hill.

Every way she turned, signs of life enhanced the atmosphere. Pausing to take snapshots of the tiny craft shop and village phone box, she returned the nods from locals and cheery grins from hikers heading off for the day. She explored a couple of side cul-de-sacs where the views across the Sound of Sleat provided postcard-worthy photo opportunities, shortening her long-legged stride as the terrain grew steeper. Further out of town, cows stopped grazing and met her gaze before dropping their heads again as if to say, 'Just another tourist'. At the sound of a tractor approaching, she pressed against the stone wall, pausing to catch her breath and return the wave of acknowledgement given by the driver.

The land opened out as she walked. Houses were left behind and white-painted stone crofts dotted the landscape. She continued up the hill to where the road faded to a narrow lane, stopping frequently to take photos.

A flock of blackface sheep appeared ahead of her, their wool long and their bellies huge. Following them, a familiar figure wearing a tartan flat cap strode quietly, an intense border collie at his heels. She stood to the side of the lane, allowing the sheep to pass before calling out a greeting.

'Good morning, Fergus!'

The man smiled. 'Good morning to you too, lassie. Took my advice I see.'

'I did. Where are you taking the sheep?'

'Home.' He pointed to a croft set back from the road a hundred metres below them. 'These have been up the road for a wee while and we're expecting a rush of new lambs in the next week or two. Time to check their health and keep them close to home.'

'Can I help?'

He stared at her for a moment, one eyebrow raised before nodding. 'After we've turned up the track, perhaps you'd close the gate behind us while Pip and I take the flock to the fank?'

She stared at him blankly for a moment. 'Fank?'

'Och. Sorry. You probably call them pens or yards in Australia.'

Ingrid fell into step beside Fergus, her eyes focused on Pip as the dog wove back and forth behind the sheep, keeping them in a tight cluster. Although of average height, she felt small next to the big Scot.

They turned into the lane, and she paused and latched the gate behind them.

About to call out goodbye, the words dissolved in her throat as Fergus said, 'I'll be having a cup of tea before we start on these. Would you like to join us?'

She hesitated for a second before accepting, uncertain who the 'us' was. Grinning, she gave him a thumbs up. *Isn't this the best way to get to know the locals?*

'I'd love to, Fergus.'

'If you care to wait by the house, I'll only be a wee while.'

While she stood in the lane, she drank in the beauty surrounding her, challenging her senses as though determined to prove the area was worth returning to. She bent over, zooming her phone camera on a butterfly she didn't recognise, when an unfamiliar male voice broke her concentration.

Her eyes widened as Fergus and a younger version of him approached. Both were of similar height, broad shouldered, and wearing the flat cap she'd noted many Scottish men wore. The younger man swung his arms as he walked, exuding energy and enthusiasm in contrast to his solemn companion.

'Callum MacRae,' he said, holding out a hand with a friendly grin. 'I came to help with the sheep but having a cup of tea with an attractive woman sounds far more interesting.'

Ingrid laughed, her insides leaping as her gaze met his. 'Father and son?'

'Not quite,' Callum said. 'Nephew.'

'Oh.' Of course! Peggy had mentioned Fergus never married when they'd chatted over breakfast that morning. Two sets of piercing blue eyes were focused on her.

'He says he doesn't need help,' Callum added, angling a sideways grin at Fergus. 'But he never sends me away when there's work to be done.'

The lines beside Fergus's eyes crinkled as if he wanted to smile but his mouth had forgotten how to. 'Ye best come inside then,' he said, throwing the door open.

A fleeting stab of nostalgia clutched her as she followed the men's example of removing their boots and hats in the sheltered porch before stepping inside. The scent of smouldering peat wafted toward them, and memories of her grandmother's stories filled her head.

Crofting was her ancestry, and this cottage was exactly the same as the home in which her grandmother had grown up decades earlier—the years before she travelled to Australia to marry the love of her life. Excitement warmed her as she adjusted from the bright sunshine to the dimly lit kitchen. She entered a forgotten moment in time.

2

———

Obeying Fergus's wave toward the table, Ingrid lowered herself into one of the four mismatching dining chairs and cast a glance around the room. A fire nestled in a white-washed nook, its warmth drifting toward her.

In addition to the small, scrubbed table, a well-worn couch pressed against the far wall while a winged, comfy-looking armchair angled toward what appeared to be a surprisingly new television. Between the couch and armchair, a tiny table provided a resting place for a teetering pile of books.

A partially open door hinted at a bedroom, the edge of a colourful quilt and a bookcase haphazardly stacked with volumes of all colours and sizes visible.

'Where do you call home?'

Ingrid returned her gaze to meet Callum's questioning one while Fergus filled the kettle and placed it on the stove. Then he too faced Ingrid as she answered.

'Queensland. A city west of Brisbane ... Toowoomba.'

'Ahh. The beautiful, sunny state we Scots long to visit,' Callum said.

Ingrid raised her eyebrows. 'Not unlike many Australians who long to check out where their ancestors came from then.'

For a few moments, conversation stalled while the tea was poured and Fergus sliced open a packet of digestive biscuits.

'I had an Australian friend once,' Fergus said, his words slow and halting as though reluctant to share them.

Ingrid and Callum simultaneously stared at him.

'What do you mean, 'once'?' Callum asked.

For long moments, silence filled the room.

'Lost touch.' He turned his head toward the fire, appearing to stare at the clock on the mantle. Rising to his feet, he reached up and shifted the clock enough to slide his hand behind it, withdrawing a sheaf of folded blue paper.

'We wrote to each other,' he murmured, staring down at the rubber-band-held bundle. 'Until she never wrote again.'

Ingrid met Callum's puzzled frown. Clearly whatever the story was with Fergus's correspondent, Callum knew nothing about it.

'What have you got there, Uncle?'

'Aerogrammes.'

Waiting for further explanation, Ingrid shuffled in her chair. When it didn't come, she asked, 'Is that some sort of letter?'

Fergus waved the bundle in front of them. 'Yes. They're letters. Not like those from the electricity company or the bank.' His voice held a hint of sarcasm. Or was it regret? 'Using one of these cost only a fraction of what a letter in an envelope would. Lightweight, one sheet of paper that folded neatly into three and included the postage. So that's what we both used. It also meant you only had a page to fill so we had to write small.'

'Or large, if I know you,' Callum said with a chuckle.

Fergus grunted, his mouth twitching. 'I might not be much of a talker, but I could still fill an aerogramme —and that was enough.'

'Who was she?' Callum asked.

Fergus stared at the clutch of flimsy letters in silence. Then, lifting his head, he turned to look through the window, his face softening. 'Her name was Lucy.'

Ingrid and Callum locked eyes. Callum shrugged.

'Are you going to tell us more?' he asked.

With clamped lips, Fergus slotted the letters behind the clock again, placed his mug in the sink, and strode toward the porch. 'I'm away to the sheep.' He stomped out, and Pip leapt to her feet from the porch mat, following him.

As the door closed, Callum shot Ingrid an apologetic grimace. 'I guess not. Sorry about that. I think I touched a nerve.'

She shook her head, disbelief and intrigue whirling in her head. 'Wow. There's a story there that sounds fascinating. And you don't know it?'

'No. He's never talked about an Australian friend before. Actually, he's never talked about any girlfriends to my knowledge. All my life he's lived alone. Here in this house, where he and my father were born.' Slowly, he rose to his feet, picked up the biscuit packet, and collected Ingrid's mug. 'Pity Mum and Dad aren't around. They'd probably know something.'

Ingrid hesitated before probing further. 'Are they on holiday?'

'Sort of. My sister lives in Cornwall. Married and had her second child a few weeks ago. Mum and Dad have gone to spend the summer with them.' He grinned ruefully. 'Not exactly Australia, but the weather down there is kinder than here in Scotland— even though the forecast is for a warmer-than-normal summer this year.'

Intrigue bubbled. Ingrid loved a romantic mystery,

and this had the potential to be as interesting as the romance novels she devoured. 'Perhaps when I get back to Australia I could see if I could track this Lucy down.'

Callum stared at her and shrugged again. 'We don't know her last name.'

Ingrid pointed to the clock. 'Would it be too intrusive to have a quick glance at the sender's address?'

A conspiratorial grin spread over his face, and Ingrid's heart thumped in her chest.

He reached for the blue bundle, turned it over in his hand, and held it out to Ingrid.

She froze. This was a private matter belonging to Fergus—a man she barely knew and one living on the opposite side of the world to her. What was she doing?

Callum gave a small nod. 'Go on. Take a photo. That way you're not guilty of leaving fingerprints—if that's what you're worried about.'

Snatching her phone from her pocket, she snapped the shot and dropped the device back into her jacket as though its disappearance signified innocence.

Callum carefully reinstated the bundle to its previous position. 'We're in this together now. Partners in crime—or international sleuths,' he finished with a wink.

She chuckled nervously, her pulse pounding, and pressed her hands to her hot cheeks. Were they burning because she'd just overruled Fergus's privacy to find his special, lost friend? Or because of the solid, earthiness of the man standing next to her, his blue eyes filled with interest and something more exciting.

Callum touched her arm lightly, angling his head toward the door. 'I'd best catch up with Fergus and get these sheep sorted out. Will you have dinner with me tonight?'

Startled at his invitation, her mind whirled with questions. Did she want to get to know this man better? Did she want a relationship—not that it had been hinted at except for attempting to solve the Lucy mystery, of course. For her, relationships hadn't worked well in the past and getting pally with a man on the other side of the world was fraught with problems. But hadn't that been exactly what her grandmother had done—and what a success that had been.

'I'd love to.'

'Grand. I'll pick you up at the pub around seven.'

Ingrid returned Callum's wave before striding out the gate. Torn between the glorious view of the sea in front of her, the invitation she had just accepted, and the address she had photographed minutes earlier, she halted beside a patch of wild flowers, opened her gallery, and stared at the photo.

Lucinda Pellegreen
"Binnalong"
Roma, Qld 4455
Australia

'Roma,' she said aloud, tilting her head as she calculated. 'Not huge and only four hours from home. That should be easy.' Hope fought with a frisson of doubt. The date stamp on the aerogramme she'd photographed was faint but the year 1990 was clear. Thirty-four years was a long time. Two years before she was born—and anything could have happened.

She turned back for another glance at the little croft housing the aerogrammes. In less than twenty-four hours, she had stepped into a home that aroused a strange sense of belonging, had met two Scotsmen who generated more than just a passing interest—and had discovered a potentially fascinating love story.

And now I have a date with the younger of said Scotsmen.

She lengthened her stride as she marched toward the village, dismissing her plans to continue her hike as her head spun with intrigue.

3

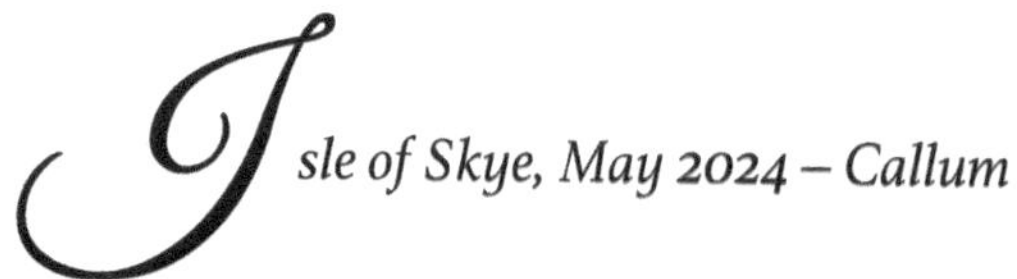

sle of Skye, May 2024 – Callum

CALLUM GLANCED at his watch as he cruised down the road. One minute to spare. He hated being late, but it had been a while since he'd dated anyone. This time though, his veins fizzed with anticipation. *I think she'll be an 'on time' girl.* There was a fine line between being early and having her get flustered, and being late, letting her think he'd forgotten.

He was right. Ingrid walked down the last two stairs, a wide smile on her pretty face as he entered the hotel.

Outside, the evening had cooled, the sky clear in the twilight.

He opened the Land Rover door for her then glanced at the drenching gun on the floor—he hastily removed it and threw it into the back seat. 'Sorry. It's been a while since this chariot has had a lady in it.'

She met his grin with a chuckle, sliding in with a dismissive flick of her hand. 'I get it. I admit my car sometimes doubles as a wardrobe—and a snack bar.'

They both laughed.

'Where are we going?' she asked.

'You'll see—it's not far and I think you'll enjoy it.'

Minutes later, she turned to him with sparkling, smoky grey eyes. 'How gorgeous!'

'Yep. It's an old hunting lodge—or was many years ago. Now it's a restaurant that features in Britain's *Good Food Guide* and has a few guest rooms for those who can afford it.'

'I see. Out of my price range then.'

He snorted. 'And mine. A friend from our school days is one of the chefs here. The food is fantastic. He reckons most of the guests come laden with binoculars and spend days deer-stalking and walking all over the estate.'

With a hand against her back, he guided her into the historic lobby. Its floors were soft with a rich tartan carpet and the walls were adorned with photos of deer and important-looking lords and ladies in tweed jackets and sturdy boots.

They sat in the corner of the restaurant overlooking the loch, muted music playing in the background, and despite the calendar depicting May as coming into summer, the crackle of the open fire warmed the room to a comfortable temperature.

Callum swilled his whisky, catching Ingrid's appreciative gaze. 'How long are you staying?'

'Sadly not as long as I would like to.'

'And how long is that?'

'I fly out of Glasgow at the end of the week. Will be back at work next Monday.'

'Oh.' Disappointment flowed through him. Today was Tuesday. Although he'd had a few girlfriends over the years, not one had intrigued him as Ingrid did. Her lithe body and gentle grey eyes oozed confidence and intelligence while her Australian accent held his undivided attention. He couldn't say why but this woman had something ... and he wanted to know her better. His uncle's secret correspondent provided the perfect opportunity.

'Yes. And I guess while I'm winging my way back 'down-under', I s'pose you'll be busy doing sheep work?'

He shook his head and laughed as the waiter came to take their order.

With their gourmet decisions made and a bottle of wine served, they were alone again and he continued, 'Although I have a small flock of my own, I'm not really a sheep farmer. I help my father and uncle when I can though and have learned the art of shearing which saves us all costs that are higher each year.' He grimaced.

'So what else do you do?'

'Build and maintain websites.'

He grinned at her wide-eyed gaze. Like most people when he first met them, especially in Ardvasar, his income-earning path surprised her. 'Most of us who grew up on Skye have left for a while—or for good. I went to Edinburgh University and studied computer science and software engineering. Worked for a couple of years in the city and hated it. I came home when Dad had a fall and broke his leg. Stayed for Christmas and haven't gone back!'

She smiled at him, strands of her blonde hair glowing gold under the subdued lighting. 'Oh.'

He leaned forward, his elbows resting lightly on the table. 'What about you?'

'I'm a nurse.' Her shoulders slumped. 'This is my first holiday in over four years—which is why I'm reluctant for it to end.' She gave a half-hearted chuckle.

'How come?'

'Not enough staff and too much work. It started with Covid really. Hospitals were so busy that we worked longer hours than ever before and as it went on, a huge number of our more experienced nurses burned out and took long-service leave or retired.' Fiddling with the cutlery, her gaze met his. 'I love my job—and I don't even mind the shift work. But I know how they felt and eventually I started to feel the same. So, I decided before it affected me enough to suffer health issues, I would do what I've wanted to do for years—visit my grandmother's home country.'

'And now you have.'

She grinned. 'Yep. Now I have. Only it's almost over and I wish it wasn't.'

He lay his hand over hers. 'Yeah. I get it. How long have you been in Ardvasar?'

'This is my second day—so I've still got a lot to see!'

Their meals arrived and conversation stalled while they savoured their first few mouthfuls.

'I've got a suggestion,' Callum said.

Ingrid narrowed her eyes as she met his hopeful grin. 'Go on.'

'If you don't mind filling in tomorrow morning on your own while I finish helping Fergus with his sheep, I'll pick you up after lunch and take you for a guided tour around Skye. I know you've probably seen some of our local sights but there are more that you won't know about.' He paused, tilting his head questioningly.

'True. I read in the tourist magazine that the Point of Sleat Lighthouse is a nice hike?'

'It is.' He nodded enthusiastically before continuing. 'We could do that tomorrow then on Thursday, leave early and visit The Old Man of Storr—the geological formation that I'm sure you've seen in heaps of photos. We could visit Dunvegan Castle, Portree, and whatever else we can fit in. How does that sound?'

'Fabulous—and busy.'

'I'll get Peggy to pack us a picnic so we can do a few walks, even if they're not long—then it doesn't matter where we are, we won't be hungry.'

Callum beamed nervously at her. Was it too much? Had he overwhelmed her? Perhaps she didn't want to spend time with him at all and had only accepted the dinner invitation out of politeness?

She leaned back and laughed softly. 'That sounds fabulous. Thank you.'

Slouching into his chair, he blew out a relieved breath and silently filled his mouth with food.

With their plates empty and dessert ordered, the conversation returned to finding Lucy.

'Where will you begin?' Callum asked. 'I mean, do you know the area? Can you make enquiries legally without invading privacy laws?'

'Not sure.' Ingrid shook her head. 'I reckon I'll check social media first. See what I can find. Pellegreen is an unusual surname, so that should be a good start. Also, I've got the name of that property too. I can ring the post office in Roma and see if they'll confirm its location.'

'Yeah. But 1990? Thirty-four years ago. That's a while. Do property names ever change?'

'I'm not sure—maybe? I read somewhere that

acreages are now issued a number based on the distance from the start of the road. I think they measure in metres then divide the number by ten and round it off—something like that anyway.'

'That makes sense. With big farms being sub-divided, the postal system would have to have a more methodical way of knowing where to deliver to than a name on a gate.' He chuckled. 1990 had been an important year for his parents and for him too, considering it was his birth year.

Callum topped up their wine glasses and raised his in a toast.

'To finding the mysterious Lucy.'

Grinning as their glasses clinked, Ingrid replied, 'And to a good tour guide as we explore his homeland.'

DELIGHTED TO WAKE up to sunshine filtering through her bedroom curtains, Ingrid dressed and entered an empty dining room.

Anna was clearing tables and resetting them for lunch.

'Am I the last person for breakfast?'

Anna laughed. 'Yes. Did you enjoy your evening with Callum?'

Heat rose up Ingrid's neck.

It had been close to midnight by the time she'd

tiptoed inside. Although neither Anna nor Peggy were about, Jack, the barman who seemed to be last to leave most nights, had been sitting in an armchair in the lounge, his snores giving away both his inactivity and his location.

She had thought she'd managed to sneak into her room unnoticed, but obviously not.

'Yes, thanks.' She ordered breakfast and Anna left the room before Ingrid allowed a soft smile to play on her lips.

It hadn't been late when they left the restaurant. Callum had driven surprisingly slowly, stopping at the Armadale pier where they could look out over the water. While they talked, the slap of waves on the shore and the occasional chug of a boat's engine filtered through the open car windows, enveloping Ingrid in the comfort of a beautiful evening. Ingrid had watched pinpricks of light flickering on the mainland as the breeze increased and Callum closed the windows.

'Time to get you back, I think. The earlier I start on those sheep in the morning, the earlier I can pick you up and whisk you off on tour-a-la-Skye.'

They had both laughed.

Nearing the hotel, Callum had reached out a hand and rested it briefly on hers.

The same gut-flip that had occurred at that moment now repeated itself. She frowned, pressing a fist against her stomach. *Stop misbehaving. It was nothing more than a friendly gesture. You're working together to help solve a problem that has clearly been troubling Fergus for decades.*

Straightening her back, she gathered her thoughts and focused on her plans to visit the local craft store, ensuring she would be back by noon in case Callum finished earlier than his predicted one o'clock. The visit to the Museum of the Isles and Armadale Castle would have to wait.

But despite her attempt to focus on her itinerary and instead eat the fruit and toast Anna placed in front of her, a flutter of excitement somersaulted through her and her appetite faded away.

4

———

*I*sle of Skye, May 2024 – Fergus

FERGUS STOMPED UP THE LANE, Pip by his side and his flock of blackface sheep leaping and frisking ahead of them, no doubt in anticipation of fresh feed waiting.

He hadn't slept well, his night broken by vivid memories of a lively young woman lying against him, her warm flesh pressed to his and her thick brown hair resting on his arm. Each time he woke, she was gone. The room—and the bed, cold and empty.

Over the years, he had repeatedly stumbled through the stages of grief. At first, disbelief. She had gone—temporarily he thought, but why wouldn't she answer his letters? Then anger had surged, consuming his every thought for days, eventually followed by despair. Finally, a semblance of acceptance had over-taken his bereft mind and wasting body. With the help of his family, he had pulled himself together.

But he had never forgotten her. And he never would.

What had made him invite the Australian girl in for a cup of tea? She was just another tourist spending a few days and more money than she probably intended. Perhaps she had a desire to take a look at where her ancestors had come from? Or perhaps she was bored with what was available in her own country and was seeking change. Maybe she was escaping a broken relationship. Whatever it was, there was some-thing about her that reminded him of Lucy and his mind leapt back to the pile of aerogrammes.

He wasn't sure now why he'd showed them to her —and Callum. During the cold depths of winter, he often got them out and re-read each one in order, scouring the words for a hint of what was to come. But there was nothing. So he would fold them neatly again and place them back behind the clock.

Now I suppose I'll have Callum cross-questioning me every five minutes about her—and God only knows what the Australian girl will come up with.

Despite the annoyance pounding in his head, memories flared in hope. *What if she decides to try and find her?*

They reached the gate into a lush paddock surrounded by thick, protective walls. Commanding Pip to hold the sheep, he walked around the outside of the flock, dragged the timber-framed barrier to the side, and stood still. With a soft whistle, he nodded toward the dog. In an instant, the first of the ewes sprang through the entrance with a joyous leap, the rest of the flock following in a torrent of black and white.

With narrowed eyes, he counted them as they passed, then, satisfied, whistled the dog to him, rubbed her ears, and closed the gate.

'Good job, girl. Next thing we know the field will be full of little'uns.' He spoke aloud but softly, so only the dog and the bird flitting in the heather nearby might hear.

'Come along, Pip. Callum will be long gone by the time we get back so we can have a cup of tea and read the paper, eh?'

She wagged her tail and trotted briskly toward home.

In rhythm with his long, even strides, Fergus murmured his favourite poem to himself. Among the pile of well-thumbed poetry books stacked on his shelves, most of them remnants from a long-hidden trunk belonging to his grandparents, those written by W.H. Auden had been his favourite. He had come across it by accident, as, when reaching for another, it had fallen to the floor. It had happened a year after Lucy had left the Isle. A year of torment and worry. But when the quote leapt out at him from the yellowing page on the floor, it imprinted in his mind and had been his mantra ever since—his fiercely private one.

'If equal affection cannot be, let the more loving be me.'

With the words on his lips, he lengthened his stride and gazed across the water, remembering when he and Lucy had trod this exact path hand in hand on that final halcyon day.

5

———

sle of Skye, May 2024 – Ingrid

FLICKING HER BLONDE PONYTAIL BACK, Ingrid stepped onto the road for the umpteenth time, straining to hear the Land Rover.

When it arrived, slowing to a stop in front of the hotel, her insides buzzed with nervous anticipation.

Callum threw the driver's door open with a beaming smile, strode around the car, and bent to pick up the rucksack resting against the hotel wall. 'Yours I presume?'

She nodded and returned his smile. 'Yeah. Peggy insisted I pack a flask of tea and she's filled a container with snacks for us.'

He tipped his head back and laughed. 'Good old Peggy. Hop in.' Callum swung the vehicle in a U-turn and they headed south toward the Aird of Sleat, obligingly slowing to a crawl at Ingrid's request. She lowered the window and captured the picturesque countryside on her phone while Callum shared his knowledge.

It seemed no time before they reached a carpark, marking the end of the public road. A large metal gate was flanked by signs.

Callum switched off the engine and pointed. 'That's where we're headed.' He glanced around before flashing her a cheeky grin. 'And it looks like we'll have the place to ourselves.'

She raised her eyebrows and opened the door, breathing in the fresh sea air. Above them, fluffy white clouds scudded across the sky like misshapen blobs of cotton wool.

Holding out Ingrid's rucksack, he rested his own beside his leg. 'Let me take the flask.'

They reorganised their packs to Callum's satisfaction and Ingrid's relief. The thermos was a large one, and added to the water bottle, her jacket, the container of food and myriad of 'essentials' such as blister plasters and a mini first-aid kit, it had increased the weight to more than she usually carried for a half-day hike.

They stopped to view the walk slideshow before

passing through the farm gate and turning to continue through a smaller, wooden version.

Companionably striding side by side, they followed the rough road as it crossed the heathered moor and rose up and down the hills, offering spectacular views over the Sound and across to the mainland town of Mallaig.

Grateful for Callum's patience and relaxed guidance, Ingrid slowed, absorbed in their surroundings and picturing in her mind how the area might look in winter with the sea winds howling around and snow on the ground. She shuddered, striding on, thankful for the glorious weather—not too warm and with a gentle breeze she compared to that of a mild Queensland winter's day.

A little over an hour later, they reached a small, isolated beach edged with rocks and pretty coloured grasses. With the tide out, white sand was exposed, beckoning them to plant footprints on its pristine surface.

'Alright for a break?' Callum asked.

Ingrid threw him a wide grin. 'You bet.' She shed her rucksack and peered at the ongoing track. 'How far to the lighthouse?'

'A few minutes. We could carry on and have afternoon tea there if you prefer ...' he tilted his head slightly, 'but it's more sheltered here and you can swim if you like.'

Ingrid snorted. 'Huh! I don't think so. I'm a Queenslander—and it's gotta be a good deal hotter than it is today before you'd get me in there.' She pointed to the sea as he joined her in laughter.

'I guess so. Tea then?'

'Much more appropriate.'

They continued to the unusual steel lighthouse, and a pang of disappointment shot through Ingrid as they inspected its surrounds. In her mind, she'd expected a tall, red-and-white-painted structure like she'd seen in other places. Still, she reminded herself, it had been an enjoyable hike—and a warm, fuzzy sensation filled her insides every time she glanced at her companion.

They returned to the carpark as the breeze turned chilly. Clouds were building, the light of day fading. Ingrid slid gratefully into the warm car. She regularly walked and jogged at home, but it had been a while since she'd completed anything more challenging than an hour or two along the town paths and parks. *This is Scotland—and very different, just like my hiking mate.*

She made a mental note to put a blister plaster on her little toe tomorrow before she walked anywhere. But ignoring the minor discomforts, her heart soared. Callum was unlike any other male she'd met. Filled with local knowledge and history, he was also open and caring—traits she was familiar with in her line of work but had never experienced from her very limited love life. Without fuss, he'd waited to help her leap over wide puddles and paused to point out moist or rocky patches to be avoided. As they'd walked, he shared tales of peat bogs and ancestors calling in the night, sending shivers up her spine—until she'd met his cheeky grin and twinkle in his eyes and realised he was teasing her or perhaps testing her?

'Brave enough to spend another day with me tomorrow?' He squeezed her hand, jolting her back to the present.

Heat radiated through her, and she dared not move. His hand was warm and dry, filled with strength and promise.

'Sounds fabulous.'

He started the car as she continued, 'I forgot to ask if you got everything done with the sheep?'

'Yep. For the moment anyway. A couple of jobs in the office next—so ... I'm looking forward to tomorrow. Gotta make the most of what time you have left here because once you leave, I reckon the place will be a bit empty.'

Her heart leapt. The tone of his voice suggested a regret that she, too, felt. Was their meeting one of those 'meant to be' situations she read about in her romance novels? The dreaminess that wafted through her ended abruptly as a vision of her parents flashed across her mind. She swallowed what felt like a lump of dough in her throat. Romantic stories were great for escapism. But the heroines' lives were not those of a hard-working Australian nurse. They were purely fiction—and her life was very real.

HER LAST DAY on the Isle of Skye proved to be one she would never forget. True to his word, Callum arrived at the hotel on the dot of eight o'clock and, with Peggy's hamper on the back seat and their rucksacks in the boot, they headed north.

A diversion westward took them to the fascinating Dunvegan Castle where Ingrid could have stayed all day. The magnificent gardens and history oozing from the castle walls were like nothing she had seen before. *Mum would love this.* The sudden image of her mother surprised her. Thinking of what might be waiting for her at home had become more difficult since meeting Callum and Fergus. Despite her enjoyable fortnight in France, Austria, and Germany, visiting the Isle of Skye felt as though a new world had opened up to her. Perhaps it was because her own grandparents had come from Scotland. She couldn't remember her grandfather, but she wondered if somewhere deep within her, Fergus triggered a long-ago memory.

'Penny for them?' Callum said.

Chuckling, Ingrid shook her head. 'Sorry. Not sure what it is but I think I'm feeling my roots.' The moment the words were out of her mouth she regretted them. Would he think her stupid, or weird?

Instead of the explosive, disbelieving snort of laughter she might have expected from a past boyfriend, he studied her quietly before giving a small nod of acknowledgement. 'Highly likely. There's a lot of history in this country, some good but not all of it happy. If your family originated here, they most likely would have experienced hardship at some point. Even the very wealthy often fell on hard times when death duties had to be paid.' He paused for a moment before asking, 'Do you know why they moved to Australia?'

'I don't know much about my grandfather except that he came from Fort William. Apparently he met my grandmother in the late sixties and soon after marrying, they did what more of their age were doing back then—having a look at the rest of the world. They got as far as Australia and were working on a cane farm in north Queensland when Cyclone Tracy arrived and literally blew Darwin away.'

'What?'

'It's true—and it's nearly fifty years since that happened.'

With Callum's interest and encouragement, she shared what she had learned about Australia's worst cyclone—one that killed sixty-six people and destroyed over eighty percent of the town.

'I guess every country has its own history to tell—

and Mother Nature seems to have had a hand in a good bit of it.' He brushed light fingers across Ingrid's. 'Now, how about we head back to Portree and find somewhere to enjoy this picnic Peggy provided?'

The following hours of daylight were filled with short walks around Portree and the dramatic geological formation of The Old Man of Storr.

'It's a shame you can't stay longer. I'm sure you would love the Quiraing walk.'

'Is it far away?' Secretly, Ingrid crossed her fingers as the muscles she had challenged the day before had not fully recovered—and already the day's activities were beginning to take a toll on her energy.

'For today, yes.' He waved a hand. 'It's on the north of Skye—Trotternish.'

'Oh. Perhaps next time I come over?'

He raised an eyebrow then grinned. 'I'll hold you to that.'

BY THE TIME they reached Broadford and turned south toward Ardvasar, the blissful clear skies had clouded over and the first misty drops of rain dulled the windscreen.

'My last day here—and it looks like that's my cue. Time to go home.' She spoke quietly, an ache of regret waring against the acceptance within her.

He reached over and grasped her hand, entwining his fingers with hers. 'It's not the end. Don't forget we've got a joint project now. One that will require a lot of emails and phone calls back and forth across the world.' His eyes met hers in the half dark and she sensed the hope that matched her own.

'Before I leave in the morning, I thought I'd pop up to say goodbye to Fergus.'

'He'd like that.'

'Do you think we should ask him outright if he would mind me trying to find out what I can about Lucy's whereabouts?'

'Your call. I'll see what I can find out this end, and perhaps you can do whatever research you can in Australia. Then whatever we discover—or don't—we will share with him and see if it sparks him wanting more?'

'Good idea.' The vision of the sad man sitting at the bar with a whisky in hand flashed back. 'Why does he wear a tie when he comes to the pub?'

'I don't know. He just always has when he goes out —which is pretty much only to the pub. When my parents are here, he has tea at our house on a Sunday night, then he goes to the hotel three nights per week and stays home the other evenings.'

'Does your father wear a tie when he goes out?'

Callum guffawed. 'No. To be honest, I've never

asked Fergus his reasons—it's just something he's always done.'

'Maybe his neck gets cold and he doesn't like scarves?'

They laughed as rain drummed against the windscreen.

After parking as close to the hotel as he could while avoiding the glow of the streetlight, Callum switched off the car and drew Ingrid into his arms. As they hugged awkwardly with the gear stick between them, threatening to jab one or both in the stomach, Callum whispered in her ear, 'Can I kiss you?'

She didn't answer. Instead, she lifted her face to his, her pulse thumping.

Careful and tender, he pressed his lips against hers. She closed her eyes, relishing the precious moment, losing herself in a vortex of desire, appreciation, and need.

They pulled apart and she straightened her shoulders, their eyes meeting with mutual understanding and regret.

'Stay in touch,' Callum whispered.

'I will.' Before the urge to remain in the car became stronger, Ingrid leapt out and rushed inside, taking the stairs to her room two at a time.

I wonder if what I'm feeling now was what Fergus and Lucy felt when she left Skye. Something bad must have happened.

6

____

The rain continued overnight, and Ingrid accepted her holiday was over. It was time to return home to deal with whatever lay before her. But, as she stuffed underwear into her shoes and shoved them into the corners of her suitcase, she steeled herself to do what she knew was right and proper. As soon as she finished packing, she would drive up the hill to Fergus's croft and ask Fergus for his permission to find what she could about Lucy.

She had almost an hour before the ferry departed for the mainland. *Just enough time to say goodbye to Peggy and Anna before I talk to Fergus.*

Farewell hugs from both women surprised her. Although she tended to greet all her friends with a hug, Peggy's warm, slightly sad embrace enveloped her with more emotion than she'd expected—especially after meeting her only days earlier.

They escorted her to her car and waved a final goodbye as she drove away, heightening the aching sense of regret that clung to her.

The gate was closed at Fergus's croft, so she parked close to the stone wall, narrowly avoiding scraping the tiny, rented Volkswagen against the unforgiving granite. Then she zipped up her raincoat and stepped out into the thick drizzle.

Before she had a chance to knock, Pip barked and the door opened suddenly. She took a step back. Tipping her head, she met hooded blue eyes. The grey hairs in Fergus's eyebrows and temples shone white under the porch light, contrasting with his tanned face.

'Hello, lassie.'

'Hello, Fergus.' Her confidence plummeted. Their last encounter had ended abruptly, but she understood why. Her visit had encouraged him to share something he was likely now regretting—even though it hadn't really been her fault.

'I thought I'd come and say goodbye ... and thank you for inviting me in the other day.'

'You're leaving today?'

She nodded. 'In a few minutes.'

'And Callum? I hope he showed you the best of our island.'

'Oh yes. We've had a wonderful time together.

Umm, walking and stuff.' Her voice faded. For a few seconds she wasn't sure if it was her heart that was thumping noisily, or the sound of water dripping off the roof and running down her back.

'You'd better come in out of the weather.' Fergus retreated into the doorway.

'Thank you. B-but I haven't really got time.' She twisted her fingers together and swallowed. 'Callum and I said goodbye last night but before I leave, I wanted to ask your permission to try and locate your friend ... if you don't mind?'

'Mind? I can't imagine why you would want to go chasing down rabbit holes looking for someone who is obviously dead or who doesn't want to be found. Why would I mind?'

She flinched at his words, despite them being said more with bewilderment than annoyance.

Biting her lip, she shook her head slowly. 'I'm sorry. I found it very sad when you showed us the aerogrammes. I know I'm interfering but just thought I might be able to help.'

His face softened. 'You're a strange one. If my letters couldn't find her all those years ago, I doubt you'll have any luck now.' He grunted. 'But if you want to go on a wild goose chase, I can't stop you.'

Ingrid straightened her back and smiled. While he appeared defeated, his eyes twinkled. Was it hope?

'Thank you. I'll keep in touch with Callum, so you'll hear if I find anything.'

He nodded, his eyes alight with intrigue. 'Right then. Have a good trip home.'

She shot him another grin. 'Thanks again. Bye.'

He remained in the doorway while she reached the car and did what felt like a ten-point turn in the narrow lane under his gaze.

Then she beeped the horn and waved.

Even through the rain, Fergus's face seemed brighter now, more like Callum's handsome one. She had a full day ahead of her—catching the ferry to Mallaig, then driving to Fort William, checking the car in to the hire company, and catching the train to Glasgow before making her way to the airport. If she missed her flight, her mother would be devastated.

Her eyes burned as a lump formed in her throat, threatening to choke her.

She had said goodbye to Europe, London, and even Edinburgh without a backward glance. Why was it that here, in this tiny village at the bottom of a Scottish Island, she wanted to shut the rest of the world away and stay forever?

A dark-coated figure stepped out in front of her at the T-intersection and she jammed on the brakes, her chest pounding.

Phew. That was close. Taking a deep breath, she chided herself for losing concentration, changed into low gear, checked for traffic and pedestrians, and eased the little car toward the ferry terminal.

Fifteen minutes later and grateful for the rain camouflaging her tears, she watched the outline of Skye disappear into the mist, her heart heavy as the ferry pulled away from the pier.

I'll be back. And when I find Lucy, I'll bring you good news—I'm certain of it.

LAURA, Ingrid's sister-in-law and friend, enveloped her in a hug in the Brisbane airport arrival lounge. Ingrid clung to her before drawing apart and sharing a tired smile. While they ambled to the car, Ingrid fielded the barrage of questions, mostly requiring only one-word answers, for which Ingrid was grateful.

'You'll feel better after a cuppa and a chance to stretch your legs before you head home.'

'How do you think Dad is?'

They exited the Airport Link tunnel before Laura answered, 'Honestly, I don't know what to think. His deterioration is more rapid than I expected—but you're the nurse and I'm not, so Rod and I are looking forward to your assessment once you've seen him.'

Ingrid sighed, her heart heavy and her visions of Skye rapidly floating away. Despite the close bond between the members of her family, Rod was a busy engineer living and working in Queensland's largest city. What time he had to spare was precious and, understandably, was mostly spent with his gorgeous wife Laura and their two daughters.

Laura glanced across at Ingrid, meeting her gaze. 'The girls have gone to the park with Rod. They're excited about seeing you again and wanted to come to the airport with me. But … I thought you might need time to prepare yourself before they bombard you with questions and hugs.'

'Thank you. They'll be fine. I'm gasping for a decent cup of tea.'

Laura pressed the automatic door opener as they turned into the driveway of a large and gracious Queenslander, its veranda above the garage draped in hanging baskets filled with petunias and ferns. 'First stop will be getting the kettle on.'

Ingrid chuckled.

Less than an hour later, the high-pitched tone of excited children penetrated her slightly more alert senses.

'Aunty Ingrid. Aunty Ingrid, we're home!' a little voice shrieked.

She reached out her arms and gathered her nieces into a group hug, struggling to sit on the sofa as the three of them became entangled and fell in a laughing heap.

As excitement died down, Laura produced a salad,

platter of roast chicken, and a cottage loaf of fresh-baked bread. The family gathered around the dining table, their conversation initially filled with what the girls were enjoying at school, questions about Ingrid's trip, and the plans for the family holiday to see the dinosaur trail at Winton later in the year. Eventually, Ingrid braced herself for the inevitable.

'Mum's struggling,' Rod said.

Ingrid stared at him for a few seconds. Since the first diagnosis of their father's dementia, Rod had been the one denying there was anything wrong. 'He's just overworked. Getting older and a little forgetful. Nothing more', he'd insisted. It had been Ingrid who had sat with him and explained all she knew about how the disease could manifest itself and what they needed to prepare for. But it hadn't worked, and Rod had continued to bury his head in the sand. Until now it seemed.

'And Dad?'

Rod shrugged. 'I've been trying to visit every couple of weeks. Didn't think he was too bad until last weekend—and he wasn't really. At least not while I was there. But Mum's lost a heap of weight and looks terrible.'

'Poor Mum.' Fifteen years younger than her husband, Vonnie Sloane had frequently been mistaken for Ingrid's sister. But, after years of nursing, Ingrid was acutely aware that stress and responsibility can age a person rapidly. A stab of guilt pierced her as she remembered she hadn't turned her phone off flight mode.

Ingrid grimaced. 'I'd better switch my phone back on. Mum's probably been trying to ring me.'

Laura shot her a sympathetic look, creases appearing on her smooth, perfectly made-up complexion. It seemed even a talented beautician couldn't always hide a frown.

'I'm sorry your holiday has to end with such a burden for you.' Laura rested her hand on Ingrid's. 'Leave it off until you get home. If your mum rings here, I'll tell her your ETA will be six o'clock. How does that sound?'

A twinge of unexpected fear lurched in her gut as she reached for the mug of tea Laura placed in front of her.

'Thank you. I'll drink this then I'll be gone.'

They exchanged a mutual nod of understanding, and Ingrid swallowed the hot liquid as her heart plummeted.

7

Heading west to the Great Divide, the setting sun flashed through the windscreen, momentarily blinding her. She slowed, dropped the sun shield, and held a hand in front of her face.

It'll be gone in a few minutes, she reassured herself as she tucked behind a large truck. As the range drew closer, a golden glow formed over the top of the darkening bush and she switched on her headlights. She loved this time of day—the cool air and muted colours of autumn. But after a month of lingering twilight and short nights, she felt strangely out of place.

Reaching the top of the range, she swung right and entered the pretty tree-lined street where her parents' nineteen-sixties brick home stood—and where she would now live for however long it took.

Surprised when her mother failed to meet her at the door, Ingrid hauled her suitcase out of the boot and let herself inside.

'Please?' her mother's frenzied wail greeted her from somewhere down the hallway. The bathroom?

Ingrid dropped her gear on the living-room floor and trod quietly toward the sounds of splashing and moaning, dread gripping her already fragile stomach.

As she reached the bathroom, she froze at the scene in front of her. In the weeks she had been away, her mother appeared to have faded from a stylish and well-groomed almost-sixty-year-old to a thin, haggard woman whose unkempt hair and half-buttoned blouse appeared more like someone in their eighties.

But it wasn't only the shock of seeing her mother in such disarray—it was the man sitting in the bath with his back to her. He'd always been thin but in a fit, healthy way. The body in the tub was of someone with wasted muscles and every bone outlined against the thin skin.

'Ingrid!'

The woman flung her arms around her daughter, pressing her soaked chest against Ingrid's.

'Mum? What's happening?'

'I can't get him out of the bath. He just won't stand up.'

For a few seconds, Ingrid's dull, tired mind fought

to establish why. Then reality hit and the years of experience in all aspects of nursing flooded in.

She stepped closer and met the face that she had loved her whole life. The face of the man who had smiled and kissed her goodnight as a child. The one who'd encouraged and chased after her on the brand-new bike when she was young. And the one who had proudly stood beside her for a photo as she held the rolled parchment and hoped the mortarboard wouldn't blow off after receiving her degree.

This man was barely recognisable. The vacant stare. The thin face and the awful pallor.

Focusing on his eyes in the hope recognition would return—and out of respect for his modesty—she reached out and took his hands.

'Come on, Dad. Time to get out of the bath.'

The blank expression on her father's face didn't alter. And neither did his refusal to move. Ingrid coaxed him in a gentle but positive tone. She pulled the plug out, releasing the last vestige of privacy, wrapped him in towels, and with her mother's help, eventually lifted him onto the chair that, before she went away, she'd insisted be kept in the bathroom to assist with his rapidly declining strength.

Later, with her father tucked up in bed after a gruelling episode of trying to get him to eat, the two women sat in the lounge, the television showing an unrecognisable program that neither were watching.

'I'm sorry, Mum.'

'Darling, we weren't to know his decline would be so fast. You needed a holiday and I'm glad you managed that. But ..." She stared at Ingrid, her eyes glistening with unshed tears and her voice breaking. 'What do we do?'

'The doctors did say it was a rare type of Alzheimer's. Unfortunately, it seems everything is happening much faster than we imagined.' Ingrid's shoulders drooped. Her whole body felt heavy—as though someone was sitting on her, preventing her from drawing a proper breath. *Poor, poor Dad.* Anger flared inside her. Why did it have to happen to an intelligent, fit, and vibrant man? A brilliant teacher and a loving husband and father?

'So, what should we do?' her mother repeated.

Ingrid moved closer to her mother and held her hands. 'We cope. I don't have to return to work until tomorrow's night shift, so we'll make an appointment first thing to see the doctor again and take it from there. While we wait, I'll unpack my stuff, we'll care for Dad, and be as normal as we can be.'

Although she didn't voice it, the moment the doctor saw her father, Ingrid knew the ball would begin rolling for home help—respite care or whatever was available. The problem was, with her job consuming most of her time, especially now she had taken leave and would be expected to backfill shifts with short staff, how would her mother cope?

As a tear rolled down her mother's face, Ingrid wrapped Vonnie Sloane in her arms and held her tight. How had she managed to talk so brightly to Ingrid each time she had called home? Ingrid prided herself on being observant—and that meant picking up on things others may miss. How had she not recognised that even her mother's usual bubbly self was quieter, less enthusiastic than normal?

Because I was happy.

A wave of guilt washed over her. Jet lag and gut-wrenching despair added to her load. Tears streamed down her face and dripped onto Vonnie's blouse.

The memory of being held—kissing Callum MacRae only two days earlier—flashed across her vision as she sobbed.

Eventually, pulling herself together, she released her mother and wiped her face on her sleeve. All thoughts of the two blue-eyed men from the Isle of Skye and tracing Lucy Pellegreen would have to wait. She wasn't sure how or what she would tell Callum when she eventually found time to email him. But her father's illness must now be her main focus. It was her responsibility to be there for both her parents.

And it was her worst nightmare.

8

———

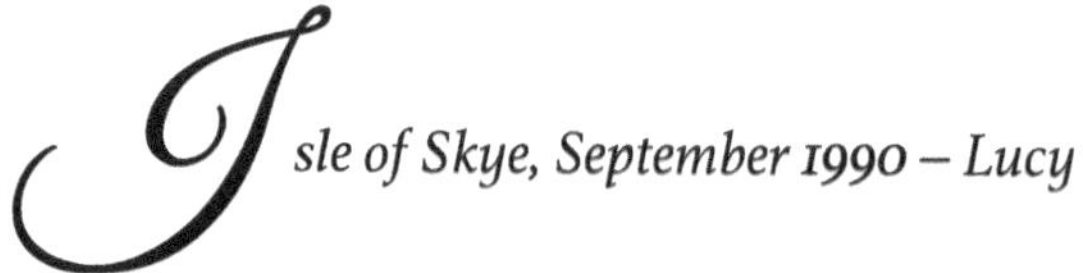

sle of Skye, September 1990 – Lucy

FERGUS BRUSHED a gentle hand over Lucy's wavy brown locks.

'What do you think?'

The answer spread across her face—an elated smile, sparkling green eyes, and the kiss she planted on his lips. 'It's fabulous. And it will be yours?'

'Not mine, ours.'

Her smile widened. 'Are you sure Granny wants this?'

'Aye. She's looking forward to living with Mum and Dad—and given she's been there for months now anyway, she might as well make it permanent.'

Lucy chuckled. 'Most of the older generation are reluctant to leave their homes. She's the opposite.'

'It was the fall she had a few months back that changed her. Lucky she and Mum get along so well.' He pulled her against him. 'And it's great that Neil and Shauna have settled into the annex and don't want to move again. With Mum and Granny next door, they won't be short of a babysitter for wee Callum either—and we can be alone.'

Lucy's delighted grin met his. 'So, everyone is happy, especially us.'

'They are—and this is the perfect opportunity for me to introduce you to your new home.'

She squealed as he swept her up in his arms and kicked the door open.

After he lowered her to the floor, they remained silent as they cast their eyes around the main living area.

'It could do with renovation, but that's even better,' Fergus said, noting the worried frown creeping across Lucy's face. 'We'll make it exactly the way we want it to be. Granny hasn't allowed anyone to do a thing since Grandpa died, but I think her grieving days are behind her now and I'm sure she would be happy for us to make it our own.'

'Good,' Lucy said tentatively. 'Now I just have to tell my parents about us getting married over here.'

She nibbled her bottom lip; a sign Fergus was coming to understand she did when worried.

'Don't think they'll approve?'

Lucy shook her head. 'It's not that. It's just that they'll probably think we haven't known one another long enough. That and the fact that Mandy and I are their only children. No boys to take over the farm, and Mandy has made it very clear she has no interest in farming. She hardly ever comes to see Mum and Dad anymore—too tied up with her job and life in Brisbane.'

'Would they really expect you to take over the farm though? I mean, you've spent years of study to become a registered nurse. Surely they wouldn't want you to give that up?'

'They don't. But that was one of the reasons I decided on nursing, along with every second country girl in my class. With the shift work involved, it's something I could do and still help on the farm. Anyway, both Mum and Dad are fit and well so it'll be years before I would have to think about it.'

'Okay.' He glanced at his watch. 'You'd better get back to the hotel if you're helping with the catering for tomorrow's ceilidh.'

'And you'd better get down to the village hall and help set up.'

They joined hands as they walked to Fergus's mud-splattered Land Rover. Fergus opened the passenger door. Reaching out with both hands, Lucy clasped his stained farm shirt and raised her face to his.

'When shall we tell everyone?'

He tilted his head and quirked an eyebrow. 'I'd like to tell the whole world right now. But ... let's get the ceilidh over with first and then ring your parents. Once we've done that, I'm sure all we'll have to do is tell Granny and the whole island will know within hours that Fergus MacRae and Lucy Pellegreen are engaged.'

Laughing, they hugged briefly before climbing into the vehicle.

'This year's end-of-summer ceilidh will be one we'll never forget,' Fergus said. 'And every year when it comes around again, we'll dance and remember our commitment to each other.'

Lucy tipped her head back and laughed—a warm, hearty laugh filled with joy.

'I can't wait.'

GREETING Lucy and Fergus as they walked through the door, the lively music—a combination of old Celtic folk tunes and more modern songs played on fiddle, accordion, tin whistle and bodhran—ensured everyone was swinging around the room or toe-tapping as they sat and watched.

It had been a hectic day. For Lucy, the Ardvasar

Hotel kitchen had buzzed with activity as food was prepared for the ceilidh as well as catering for in-house guests. Although she enjoyed nursing, her decision to travel for a year had been a good one. Months of seasonal work in the hotel had given her a change of occupation she had enjoyed—and now the thought of returning home to outback Queensland had been exceeded by the excitement of making a new home here on Skye with her gorgeous Scottish farmer.

Next week, I'll start applying for nursing jobs here.

Her insides flipped with excitement and a touch of trepidation. What if she couldn't get work over winter? If the little hospital in Broadford was already fully staffed? Her savings wouldn't last forever and the last thing she wanted was to be dependent on Fergus—at least before they were married.

'Come on.' Fergus grabbed her hand and swung her into the melee of dancers.

Her skirt flared as they spun around the room and when the music stopped, she leaned against his chest and drew breath. He smelled of soap and fresh air. Stepping back, their gazes met and she smiled.

'It looks great,' she said, reaching to straighten his tie.

Although almost no-one else wore one, they had joked that wearing a tie to special occasions was something the aristocracy would do—and in Lucy's eyes,

Fergus was king and should therefore heed to traits of one 'to the manor born'.

When he had protested initially, she'd said, 'You're special though,' so he'd agreed to wear the only one he had—'Just this once'. It was a bright shade of blue that had matched the bridesmaids' dresses at Neil and Shauna's wedding, and although he didn't acknowledge it, the colour perfectly matched his eyes.

Halfway through the evening, the band took a break and supper was spread on a long table in the side room of the hall.

'I'm famished.' Fergus passed Lucy a plate and began loading his with a mini-meat pie, a Scotch egg, stovie, bacon butty and a piece of tea cake.

Lucy elbowed Fergus in the ribs as her own stomach growled. She hadn't eaten since lunch, choosing to spend her off-duty time washing her hair and ironing her clothes for the evening. Now her mouth watered at the sight of the traditional dishes she had come to love.

'Save some for me.'

He chuckled and passed her the plate of Scotch eggs. 'Your favourite.'

'Yum.' She took one and they moved away from the table as Neil and Shauna approached.

'Are you enjoying your first ceilidh, Lucy?' Shauna asked.

'Loving it.'

They had to raise their voices as conversations around them increased in volume, enjoyment reaching a peak as drinks flowed and food was eaten.

'Callum alright?'

'Aye. He enjoys being with his granny and grandpa—and they're happy to miss this year's dance.'

The two women drifted closer to the table again, and Lucy reached for a cranachan, a delicious raspberry and cream dessert. 'I think we made eighty of these this morning, so I believe I should do a taste test.'

Shauna laughed and helped herself to one before leaning closer to Lucy. 'I've never seen Fergus this happy. You two make a great couple—and that has nothing to do with you being able to shear sheep.'

Lucy exploded with laughter. Growing up surrounded by the woolly creatures, she had laboriously followed her father's instructions when, at age twelve, she had shorn her first pet lamb. Fortunately, the poor animal was eventually de-robed of his wool as between her having to re-grip the heavy, vibrating electric handpiece and rearranging the protesting lamb between her knees, it had taken much longer than it should have. Now, another twelve years on, she was still slow but had mastered the knack and had proudly challenged Fergus to a two-sheep speed-shearing competition a few weeks earlier.

'Yeah. That was just luck. With the woeful price of

sheep at home now, my parents have switched to cattle so it's a while since I've even held a handpiece.'

'Well, you certainly impressed Neil—he hasn't stopped talking about it and I've told him in no uncertain terms not to even think about me learning. The whole family are hoping you're not considering returning to Australia too soon?'

Her heart skipped a happy beat. She and Shauna had connected from the beginning, having met the week Lucy had arrived in Skye to work for the summer season in the hotel. Shauna's pregnancy had been evident and so was her welcoming nature. Within minutes of them meeting, Lucy had found herself accepting an invitation to Shauna's baby shower, a farm visit—'So you don't get too homesick', and the local book club's weekly meeting—'If you can get the evening off work'.

The band started up again and the crowd drifted away from the food tables and back onto the dance floor.

It was hours later before Lucy and Fergus meandered arm-in-arm up the road in the cool autumn air. Above them, a full moon cast its light on the gentle waves while the sound of small boats nudged the wooden pylons with soft clunks.

The music had ceased, and the air was filled with cheery goodbyes—and slurred words of protest from those who had overdone the celebration and were now being manhandled into vehicles.

'This time next year we'll be walking up that hill to our own wee croft,' Fergus said, wrapping his arm more tightly around Lucy.

They paused, kissed, and then ambled on before stopping again and repeating the process.

A few metres from the hotel, a door slammed and Peggy, the young, newly appointed manager of the hotel, stepped into the lamplight. 'Lucy! Is that you?'

'Yes, it is.' Lucy's stomach did a somersault at Peggy's tone, high-pitched with anxiety.

'Quick. It's your sister. On the phone.'

The two of them ran the final few metres, with Fergus closing the hotel door behind them.

'In the office,' Peggy directed.

Lucy picked up the receiver, turning a pale, fearful face toward her beautiful new friend and supervisor—and the man she loved. Her sister had never phoned her before. Or written. 'Hello?'

'It's me, Mandy. You have to come home.'

'Why? Is something wrong?'

'Yes. Mum's had a stroke.'

Lucy froze as the bottom fell out of her world.

9

———

Collapsing onto the office chair, Lucy fought to absorb her sister's words.

'Serious. Airlifted to Toowoomba Hospital. I'm with her now ... things don't look good. You're the nurse. You HAVE to get on a plane—now!'

Finding her voice, Lucy whispered, 'I'll let you know my flight details as soon as I can.' Then she replaced the receiver and stared at the two worried faces in front of her.

'It's Mum. She's had a stroke. I have to go home.'

Fergus's face turned ashen, his eyes filled with silent horror. For long seconds, their gazes met as both absorbed the implications—while the joy and excitement of the evening that had just been, faded into oblivion.

Peggy clasped Lucy's hands. 'Of course you must.

Your family need you.' She turned to glance at Fergus. 'And we'll be here to welcome you back when everything in Australia returns to normal again. Now, I suggest we have a nice hot drink and get some sleep. In the morning, bring whatever documents you need and use the office phone to ring the travel agency and make a booking.'

In a daze, Lucy allowed Fergus to wrap his arm around her and lead her into the kitchen where Peggy bustled about and placed a mug of hot chocolate in Lucy's hands.

An hour later, reality set in and Lucy's eyes prickled with tears.

Peggy rose, rinsed her mug, and placed a gentle hand on Lucy's. 'Things will look better in the morning. Try and get some sleep and we'll talk again then.'

She nodded as Peggy turned to Fergus.

'Lock the back door when you leave please, Fergus.'

'Of course.'

They waited until Peggy had left the room before Lucy spoke.

'Will you stay with me tonight?'

'I will.' He glanced toward the kitchen and shot her a soft smile. 'I'll just lock the door.'

IN THE PRE-DAWN LIGHT, the clouds cleared, allowing a silvery glow to penetrate the glass, pooling on the feather quilt and illuminating the couple bound together, her back against his chest and his arm holding her tightly to him.

Later, a watery sun slanted through heavy clouds as they dressed. Lucy extracted her passport and credit card from her suitcase and leaned against Fergus for a long minute. Then, retracing their steps to the office, they quietly slipped past the kitchen where Peggy and Dee, the New Zealand girl who had arrived only a week earlier to help out until the end of the season, were engaged in a muted conversation. Lucy ran her finger down the pages of the office phone book, stopping at the number for the local travel agent. Fiona had become another of Lucy's friends since they'd met earlier in the year at the village book club. A bright, well-travelled local girl, her experience and willing attitude had been welcomed by the new owner of the Broadford Travel Agency and although it was the weekend, Fergus assured her Fiona would pull out all stops to get Lucy on a flight.

Fergus fidgeted, his gaze repeatedly focused outside. It had been their plan to get the ewes and lambs in while the weather held. September not only signalled early autumn, but it was also the time to wean the almost full-grown lambs from their mothers.

Days earlier, she and Fergus had checked and

repaired the fences and stone walls, ensuring the paddocks on the croft were secure. Weaning was a noisy, stressful time for both mothers and lambs, and if given half a chance, the youngsters would seek out a weak spot in their prison and break out.

'Leave it with me,' Fiona said in a compassionate but efficient tone. 'There are flights from London, but I'll see what I can find from Glasgow and call you back.'

'Thanks, Fiona. I'll be waiting.'

Lucy rose and crossed the room to Fergus, leaning her head against his broad chest for a moment before lifting her eyes to meet his. 'I'm not expecting a flight for at least a day or two, so why don't you go and bring the sheep in as planned. As soon as I've got the details, I'll talk to Peggy and then join you. It's my day off anyway and there's only a couple of guests staying, so I'm sure Peggy and Dee will be fine.'

Nodding, he gave her a quick hug and was gone.

As his familiar masculine scent, enhanced with a whiff of Ralph Lauren's "Polo" aftershave, wafted out the open door, Lucy lay her forehead on folded arms and rested on the desk. *If only phone calls weren't so expensive.* Emails were in their infancy, unavailable for the average person, and while sending a telegram would arrive in Australia quickly, it wouldn't be enough. A letter was out of the question. Mandy was demanding an answer—and assistance—*now!*

She drew a deep breath and slowly released it. She would simply have to forfeit half her week's pay and tell Peggy to use the money to cover the cost of her phone calls.

Unsure how long she sat there, Lucy must have dozed off as at the shrill ring of the phone, she jumped, banging her knees against the underside of the desk. She snatched up the receiver. 'Ardvasar Hotel, Lucy speaking.'

'It's Fiona, Lucy. I've got you on a flight from Glasgow to Brisbane tomorrow afternoon. Departure at four-thirty, so you'll need to be at the airport by two o'clock. Can you do that?'

'Sure. Fergus will drive me, and we'll go on the Mallaig ferry. Oh wait, what about the ticket and how do I pay for it?'

'Because of the urgency, I've arranged for our head office to issue the ticket and take your credit card payment when you get to the airport. They've got a desk there. The lady's name is Melinda—she'll have a name tag on and will be wearing the same uniform I do so you can't miss her. Just make sure you've got your passport handy, and she'll help you complete the departure forms if you need it. I'm sure everyone will help you.'

'Thanks, Fiona. I'm truly grateful—and once I know what's going on in Australia and can come back, we'll get together for a drink sometime, yeah?'

'Sounds great. Good luck now.'

After hanging up the phone, Lucy stared at it in silence. Was this whole thing real? Had she really received a call from Mandy and had her vibrant, forty-seven-year-old mother really suffered a stroke? She was too young. Too fit.

Anger rose inside her and mingled with the pain of loss—not only the loss of her mother's health, but the loss of togetherness and the new, passionate and exciting relationship she and Fergus had just begun.

OUTSIDE, laughter sounded as two teenage girls walked by, seemingly without a care in the world. *I wonder if they're sisters? Huh, if they are, they're better friends than Mandy and I were.* Lucy's mind drifted, still struggling with the reality of her situation.

Mandy had sounded pretty stressed and upset on the phone—quite unlike her usual composed self. Memories of years past flittered through her head.

With two years separating them in age, it might as well have been ten. Mandy's serious, controlling attitude and her distaste for farm life had ensured she remained an "inside" girl as they grew up—more willing to vacuum the floors and assist her mother in the kitchen while Lucy had adored being outside helping their father. Their constant arguing when sharing a bedroom had eventuated in having a whole new wing added to the farm homestead, providing a much larger bedroom and ensuite for their parents and allowing the girls to each have their own room.

When Mandy had left home for boarding school, Lucy had revelled in her absence. She'd known it wasn't exactly the right feeling to have for her only sister, but at least she could get to the shower when she wanted to, listen to the country music she preferred instead of boring jazz and orchestral stuff—and have her two best friends, Helen and Roslyn, come and stay the weekend without Mandy's disapproving stares and constant complaints that they were too noisy.

Somehow the bond her parents had wanted the girls to have had never quite eventuated. But now, in the midst of her mother's health crisis, it was clear that Lucy needed to put her childhood behind her and be the support crew she knew her father and sister would need.

DRAFTING ewes from lambs was exactly the distraction Lucy needed but even so, it was hard to concentrate and more than one lamb slipped past her before she slammed the gate. Without a word, Fergus climbed over the fence, snagged the lamb, and ushered it into the correct pen.

'Sorry.' Lucy bit back tears. 'I'm not being very helpful.'

Fergus's sun-weathered face softened as he ran a hand through his dark hair. 'It's okay. You're doing a great job and we're nearly finished. We'll leave the lambs in the yards tonight with some hay and pellets. Then we'll take their mums up to the common. The walk will do us both good and we can talk about tomorrow.'

He was right. With a soft breeze blowing from the sea behind them and Jet, Fergus's dedicated border collie, weaving back and forth keeping the sheep together, they trudged hand in hand up the hill and along the ridge.

'We'll write to each other every week and as soon as your mum's well enough, you can tell her about us getting married—then perhaps they'll come back with you for our wedding?'

She squeezed his hand and choked back a sob. *Why, why is this happening? Fergus and I have a whole new life ahead of us. Like nursing at the village hospital, doing up Granny's cottage—and working on the croft together.*

Life had looked so good. Perfect even—until now.

ueensland, September 1990 – Lucy

THE LONG, gruelling flight back to Australia provided more than enough time for Lucy to reflect on her six months living on Skye—and her love for Fergus.

A tingle of amazement swept over her as she peered through the aircraft's window at the never-ending sky. Following an exhausting four years of both study and working in the local medical centre between university stints, then a further year of full-time nursing with no more than roster breaks, it had been her mother who had suggested she needed a holiday—one of travel and opportunities in places other than Australia.

The bus tour across Europe had been fun—sort of. With thirty-three other Australians and New Zealanders for company, there was no way she could be lonely. But within the first week, she accepted she was not like every other travelling twenty-four-year-old. She had two arms, two legs, and a good brain, but in every other way, she felt like a square peg trying to fit into a round hole. Party life had never been her "thing" and that was exactly what the bus tour seemed to be. One eight-week-long party as they negotiated windy roads, glorious snow-capped hills and mountains—and a lot of cheap hotels. Exhausting, noisy, and ostracising for those who wanted to make the most of exploring the beautiful buildings, churches, and countryside.

Reaching London had been a relief. She had said goodbye to her travelling companions, whipped around the obligatory "must-see" London icons, then jumped on the first train to Scotland. Arriving in Edinburgh in late March, she had added another coat to her luggage and walked for miles around the city. The youth hostel had been clean and comfortable, and she had shared with a nice Canadian girl who was enjoying her final days before returning home to enjoy a North American spring. But it wasn't where she had wanted to stay.

With the map of Scotland spread out across her narrow bed and a desperate longing to escape the crowds and noise, she had closed her eyes, thrown a coin in the air, and waited for the plop as it dropped onto the paper—right in the middle of the Isle of Skye.

Within twenty-four hours, she had reached the small town of Broadford—an exciting and scenic journey requiring several changes of trains, buses, and finally a ferry.

In the local grocery store, she had scoured the public notice board, her heart leaping when she spotted the advertisement:

"Hotel staff required for a popular hostelry in the quiet village of Ardvasar."

She'd dragged out her map again and searched for the location, eventually asking the check-out girl for assistance.

'There.' She'd stabbed a finger on the map before staring at Lucy curiously.

Is it my accent that's confusing you? Lucy had forced a smile and the check-out attendant-come-tour-guide appeared to soften.

'Just down the road a wee way. You can't miss it.'

And two hours later, she'd had a job. Not only a chance to recoup some of her savings, but one that had come with free board and lodgings, even if the wages were low. For a single Australian woman travelling alone, it had been gold.

Days later, meeting Fergus while out walking on her first afternoon off had been the happiest coincidence she could recollect ever experiencing. Had it been fate? She believed so. Driving a flock of sheep onto the common behind the village with a strong, keen-eyed border collie at his side, he had paused and turned—presumably to see who was following him. She wasn't—it hadn't been intentional. She'd wandered all over the village before striking out into the more rural areas, and it was just coincidental that he and his sheep were dawdling up the lane—and she was a fast walker.

His pleasant, if hesitant "hello" had been warm.

It had been easy to tag along with him, talking about sheep and comparing Australian ways of farming with those in Scotland. She had been disappointed when the animals had scampered toward the common land where they clearly knew there would be fresh grass waiting for them over summer.

She smiled to herself, staring unseeingly through the plane window. It had been the beginning of something special. Something she had never dreamed of—something totally unexpected.

'Would you like the chicken or beef?'

The smiling cabin-crew attendant was staring at her, and it took a few seconds for Lucy to register her question.

'Oh ... the chicken please.'

As she munched her way through the compact and tasty meal, thoughts of Fergus, their hopes and dreams, and the vision of beautiful, wild, unpredictable Skye faded, replaced by the fear that her mother may not be able to talk to her when she reached the hospital—or worse still, she would have another stroke and ...

Her appetite disappeared and as much as she tried to focus on the positive side of her mother's hospitalisation, the weight in the bottom of her stomach grew heavier.

As ARRANGED during the brief phone call between the two sisters with flight details, Mandy was waiting in the arrival area of the Brisbane Airport.

'Thank goodness you're here.' Mandy gave Lucy a quick hug before turning away. 'Come on. Visiting hours will be over by the time we get to the hospital if we don't hurry.'

Lucy blinked. No "Hello. Thanks for dropping everything and coming home." No understanding her travel-weariness and certainly no apology for interrupting her happy life in Scotland. Her shoulders sagged as she half carried, half dragged her suitcase along behind her. She was too tired and too worried for tears. Her mum was her main focus, and she shouldn't have expected any compassion from Mandy.

The hint of a smile twitched. *She must save that for her students.*

During the two-hour car journey, conversation was completely one-sided—in favour of Mandy. An occasional yes or no was all that appeared to be required from Lucy.

Understanding very little of Mandy's complicated reasons for not being able to help their mother, by the time they reached the Toowoomba Hospital Lucy had at least established that the stroke had happened while their mother had been shopping in Roma. According to Mandy, their mother's collapse in the supermarket had been fortuitous in the respect of receiving a quick response from the paramedics whose base was less than two minutes away. Lucy dreaded to think of what may have happened had they been out on the farm.

Lucy had to trot to keep up with her sister as they entered the building, stepped inside lifts, and trailed along corridors.

Hugging her father first, Lucy hastily bit back the tears that threatened as she moved to hug her mother for a long time.

'Hello, Lucinda. I'm sorry,' Leigh slurred.

Her face was lopsided and her overall appearance unlike the mother Lucy had left when she set off overseas at the beginning of the year. But Leigh was alive—and that was all that mattered.

'We're hoping Mum will be discharged sometime

in the next few days. So,' Mandy said matter-of-factly, 'I suggest tomorrow you and Dad return to the farm, Lucy, and I will stay with Mum until discharge then bring her home. I'll hang around for a further week and ensure the appropriate home care is arranged, and then it will be up to you and Dad to look after her. I have to return to my job.'

It all sounded so straightforward. Lucy's jet-lagged, weary mind absorbed only the facts, presuming the appropriate scans had been done and a plan was in place going forward. Her mother would recover, and she and her father would follow Mandy's suggestions. At least by then she would be over her jet-lag and able to give their mother her full attention.

Heaving a silent sigh, a vision of their farm flashed through her head. 'Who's looking after Binnalong while you're here?'

'Robert.' Lucy's father, Brent—a tall, thin man with a tanned face and twinkling green eyes the same as Lucy's—finally got a word in. 'He's feeding the dogs, checking water and what-not. Said he'll take care of things until we no longer need him.'

Lucy nodded. Robert, the youngest of four brothers from Dalgonally, the property next door, was the same age as Lucy. As children, they had travelled on the school bus together and, although they each went separate ways once at their destinations, a friendship of sorts had remained. As a quiet, shy boy, Robert had seemed to enjoy Lucy's bright, outgoing company and they shared a common love of animals, especially horses.

'Okay,' Lucy said. 'Where are we staying tonight?'

'I've booked a motel close by. Dad's got the main bedroom and you can sleep in the spare bed next to mine.'

'Right.' Lucy clamped her lips together, stemming the groan that threatened. *Just like old times.*

11

———

*L*ucy frowned as she ran down the list of observations hanging on a clipboard at the end of her mother's bed.

'Has the doctor discussed the results of the MRI yet?'

Mandy straightened her shoulders. 'She hasn't had one.'

Confused, Lucy glanced at the information on the clipboard again. 'I wonder why not? It's been recommended.'

'Well, yes,' Mandy said tartly. 'It was suggested— but she would have to go to Brisbane for it and they've already done CT scans, so I felt it unnecessary. I mean, Mum has suffered a stroke. Why would they need to do more? We just want them to get on with the rehabilitation so she can go home.'

A stab of incredulity bit at Lucy. Turning to her father, she asked, 'Did you also agree?'

He shook his head, his face drooping with disappointment. 'I wasn't thinking straight, love. All I could think about was your mother, so I guess I left the decision to Mandy.' Creases knotted between his eyes. 'Why would they want to do an MRI? I thought that was only for a cancer diagnosis.'

Lucy perched on the end of her mother's bed and forced down the lump of frustration rapidly growing in her throat. In her jet-lagged state, she longed to get up and slap her sister. But ... she conceded, that wouldn't help at all.

'I'm not sure but we need to talk to the doctor about the results of the CT scans. Mandy, if it is proven to be a stroke that Mum's had, before she can be discharged, she needs to be cleared by a speech pathologist and have her fluids assessed. A one-sided facial droop like what Mum has usually means she would be on thickened fluids only.'

'Oh.' Mandy rolled her eyes.

'Right then,' Brent said firmly. 'You know better than either Mandy or me, Lucy. What do we do next?'

'I'll speak to the charge nurse, and we'll see if we can have a talk with the doctor.'

It was late afternoon and Lucy was dozing in the chair beside Leigh's bed when the doctor and charge nurse arrived.

Introductions were made and the doctor, a man with a shaved head who looked too young to be qualified, sat on the end of Leigh's bed.

'I'm pleased you're all together—and that you are a nurse, Lucy, as it is sometimes difficult for families to understand our medical world.' He shared a gentle smile, consulted his notes, and drew a deep breath. 'The scans are showing a couple of areas of concern, and we would like to send Leigh to Brisbane for an MRI.'

'Is it because of the melanoma Mum had removed from her back last year?' Lucy asked.

'I told the other doctor yesterday that she'd had a skin cancer,' Mandy said tartly.

'Melanoma is very different to skin cancer,' the doctor said calmly. 'While Leigh has suffered symptoms we normally relate to a stroke, it would be prudent to clarify exactly what the cause of her condition is. That's why we consider it appropriate to send her to Brisbane for an MRI. It is a full body scan that will clearly show us where any problems are. Once we have that information, treatment, if required, can be discussed and instigated.'

He looked up at Brent who swung his gaze in turn to Lucy and Leigh.

Leigh nodded and spoke slowly and carefully as if trying to prove there was nothing dramatically wrong. 'It sounds like a good idea. When?'

'Nurse Stubbs will contact them and get back to you with a date and time. Unfortunately, we don't have many MRI scanners in Queensland yet, so there may be a few days' wait.'

'Thank you,' Brent said. 'Should we stay here until then?'

The doctor scanned his notes again. 'If you mean, stay in Toowoomba, that's really over to you. Leigh will be well cared for and if you need to return to your farm, then please don't worry. We will contact you if her condition changes in any way—and of course you are welcome to phone each day and speak to her. Each of our wards now has a phone.'

They shared their thanks, and the nurse and doctor left the room.

Slumping onto the bed, Brent picked up Leigh's hand and stroked it gently. 'What would you like us to do, love?'

'Go home,' she said. 'As the doctor says, I'm fine here and it's Saturday tomorrow so we know it's unlikely the MRI will happen in the next couple of days. It could be a week.'

'I hope not, Mum,' Lucy said. 'Hopefully, we'll know something in the next half hour.'

Leigh was right. The appointment was made for the following Tuesday. Brent gave the appropriate authority and documents were signed.

Mandy perched on the edge of the chair beside the bed, her hand holding her mother's as though acknowledging she may have been quick to make such important decisions.

Apologising had never been Mandy's way, but Lucy accepted that at least she had taken her suggestions without argument.

'I'll sit with Mum for a while and you two can go to the motel and have a rest if you like.'

'Thanks, Mandy. I'd love a nap, but I might not wake until tomorrow.' She gave her sister a small smile. 'So, how about Dad and I go to the motel and have a cuppa and something to eat? Then we can come back and spend some time with Mum before bedtime.'

Nodding her agreement, Mandy picked up the magazine from her mother's bedside cabinet and flicked through the pages.

A tiny smile hovered on Lucy's face at her sister's dismissal. Turning back to her mother, she met the gentle turquoise eyes as she pressed a kiss on her pale cheek. The irregular pupils brought a sudden stab of fear to her insides and for a fleeting moment, Lucy froze. The flutter of her mother's lashes as she stared into her daughter's, suggested Leigh knew something

Lucy didn't but couldn't or wouldn't voice it. An icy chill ran down Lucy's back.

She took a deep breath, shared a smile with her family, and led her father into the corridor.

SATISFIED THERE WAS nothing more they could do, and acknowledging Leigh was in the right place, Lucy slid into the car beside her father.

'I'm sorry,' Brent said.

'What for?'

'Mandy.'

Lucy shot her father a puzzled frown. 'Why. Because she bullied you into believing Mum didn't need the MRI?'

'Well, yes ... that. And for calling you home. It wasn't necessary but you know Mandy. I asked her to phone you and explain what had happened with your mother. I never dreamt she would expect you to return at such short notice.'

Lucy reached out and lay her hand on her father's arm. 'It's okay, Dad. I'll never live up to Mandy's standards. But with Mum in this situation, I wouldn't want to be anywhere else. I can help—even if it's only to translate medical terminology so we all understand.'

Brent spluttered a half-laugh, and she grinned.

'Between us we'll muddle through,' he said. 'And

knowing your mother, it won't be long before she's up and about again.'

'Dad, you know this could be serious.'

Brent clamped his lips together and gave her a fearful glance.

A few long, silent minutes passed as they withdrew into their own thoughts.

Lucy's mind filled with doubts. She understood enough to accept recovery may not be as swift as her father and sister hoped—particularly as there had not been a confirmed diagnosis of the cause. At some point, Robert would be needed back on their own property and it would be she, Lucy, who would need to step into her mother's shoes when it came to farm work—unless they could afford to employ a farm assistant. Her mind spun off into the list of possibilities as she temporarily pushed all thoughts of Skye away.

Perhaps an agreement could be worked out between the owners of Binnalong and Dalgonally? With the highly mechanised equipment Dalgonally owned, and the absence of sheep, they might just manage with some help from next door during busy periods.

Three times the size of Binnalong, Dalgonally required at least one of the boys to remain on their property as, with each decade, profits had enabled Robert's parents to purchase more land. "Building my empire," Finlay Venables had declared at one of the cattle sales Lucy had attended with her father. So, while the middle two brothers had left, seeking careers in the mining and building industries, the eldest son, Matthew, and the youngest, Robert, had continued to work alongside their father.

She shook her head, silently chiding herself. *Forget about the farm. Your mother's medical condition is far more important.*

HAVING DECIDED to wait until the following morning before making further plans, Lucy slept heavily, only waking when Mandy began clattering around in the bedroom and the smell of coffee drifted through the doorway from the tiny motel kitchen.

'Here you are.' Brent nudged the door open and entered, clutching a mug of coffee in each hand. 'Get that down you while I make some toast, then we'll head up to the hospital and have a chat with your mum.'

With leaden limbs and a heavy head, Lucy obeyed, waiting for almost half an hour for Mandy to get out of the bathroom before she could shower and dress for the day. It was nine o'clock before hers and her father's bags were stowed in the rear of the LandCruiser and Mandy had her neat, brand-name suitcase tucked into her little Mazda.

At the hospital, Brent leapt forward and hugged Leigh.

A stab of something resembling pain but with a chord of envy ran through Lucy as she watched her parents kiss, holding each other tightly. Her mind flew to Fergus and the ache grew.

The morning tea trolley rattled down the hallway, stopping outside the ward, and a woman in a fawn-coloured uniform strode in.

Food and drinks were dispensed to the other patients in the room, and Leigh was handed a cup of thickened fluid.

'Yuck,' Mandy said, screwing up her nose. 'Is that all they're letting you have?' Her voice rose in disgust.

'Mandy. You heard what I said yesterday,' Lucy said firmly. 'It's important Mum stick to the exact diet prescribed. Until the doctor, and we, know what's going on, she can't have anything else—it could be dangerous.'

An hour dragged as Mandy huffed and protested about having to wait for the doctor to clarify details of Leigh's trip to Brisbane. While they waited, Lucy helped her mother shower and wash her hair, then sat her on a chair while she blew it dry and styled it into the familiar chestnut-coloured waves that cascaded over her shoulders.

Eventually a nurse arrived with the details of Leigh's trip to Brisbane on Tuesday.

'The ambulance will leave here at seven for the Princess Alexandra Hospital. After the MRI, scheduled for ten o'clock, she will be brought back here and the results should be available later in the day. We will let you know when the doctors can speak to you all. Okay?'

Mandy shrugged, Brent nodded, and both Leigh and Lucy shared their thanks.

After the nurse left, Leigh shared a lopsided smile with her family.

'Off you go.' She dismissed Mandy's fussing and Lucy's worried frown with a wave of her hand. 'You heard the doctor. We've got our phone in the ward so you can ring me when you're home and let me know how everything is.'

'Great.' Mandy kissed her mother perfunctorily and snatched up her handbag. With an equally brief peck on both Brent and Lucy's cheeks, she breezed toward the door with a call over her shoulder. 'See you back here next week. And Dad, make sure you ring me with the time.'

Lucy blinked and Brent gave a mock salute before turning back to his wife with a wry grin.

'Yes, ma'am. Righto, love, we'll head off and I'll ring when we're home.'

Lucy bent and hugged her mother, whispering a quiet, 'See you soon,' then they shuffled out of the room, stopping at the door to blow Leigh a kiss and share a smile.

Tears pricked Lucy's eyes as they walked away. Her mum was potentially very ill, and she hadn't even had a chance to tell her about Fergus.

And it will be at least a week before my letter will reach him to tell him what's happening.

Turning to face her father as they drove away, she asked, 'Dad, would you mind if we stopped at the post office before we leave town? I need to buy some aero-grammes.'

The empty, cream-painted homestead greeted them as they drove down the dusty driveway. With little rain all year, and nothing for the past four months, the paddocks were brown and the crops that should be ripening and standing tall were now wilted and dry. Cattle in paddocks closest to the house hung around the half-full dam and empty hayfeeders were scattered nearby. Two horses, their rugs dirty and askew, stood under a tree in the small field adjacent to the house yard, their tails flicking the endless flies. They lifted their heads as the vehicle passed by at a crawl, ears pricked and alert.

After the green of Skye, Lucy's eyes boggled. 'Gosh, it's a desert, Dad. Hello, horses!' she called through the car window.

Brent heaved a sigh. 'Yep. Barley's poor. We'll be

lucky to harvest anything. I reckon if we hadn't had the sub-soil moisture left from summer, it would be worse. Next the temperatures will soar and burn everything off if we don't get a shower soon. The weather bureau are saying we're experiencing an El Nino—which is apparently going to keep things pretty dry for the foreseeable future.'

Disbelief flooded through Lucy as her stomach cramped. She'd heard her parents talk of the drought they endured in the mid to late sixties but it had ended around the time she was born and since then, conditions had been fair to good. Now the sheep prices had slumped so low that many farmers were having to shoot them as the cost of trucking them to saleyards exceeded their value. Fortunately, three years earlier, one year before the Australian Wool Reserve Price Scheme collapsed in Australia and prices plummeted, Brent and Leigh had made the decision to increase their cattle numbers and plant more crops. The sheep had been sold and the profits poured into buying essential machinery and building a new set of steel cattle yards. The last thing the family needed while her mother was unwell was the worry and extra work a drought would bring.

'Have you got enough feed to see the stock through if conditions last a while?'

'I reckon so. The decision we made last year to plant lucerne and make hay was a good one and the irrigation setup might have been costly, but provided the electricity doesn't rise again, we'll have enough to see us through a couple of years. While you're home, perhaps you could give me a hand to wean the calves and draft off the older cows. Get them sold sooner rather than wait until the drought really takes hold.' He raised an eyebrow. 'With your mum crook and having to rush to the city, I've had a bit of time to think about what needs doing on the farm to reduce the workload, especially now she'll need us to care for her.'

They parked in the corrugated-iron shed near the house, got out of the car, and stood, their silence lengthening as they looked around. Excited barking came from under a tree between the shed and the house yard.

'I'll let the dogs off and check their food and water,' Lucy said.

'Goodo. I'll throw the horses some hay and straighten their rugs. Robert must have come early today—unless he's been too busy to feed the cattle. Ahh well, they'll be fine until the morning. I'm parched. Let's get the jobs done and have a cup of tea while the dogs have a good run around.'

In the afternoon light, Lucy's heart plummeted at the frown on her father's face. She hadn't been away a year and yet his smooth, tanned skin seemed to have shrivelled like the crops in the paddock, the creases around his eyes and on either side of his mouth now deep, giving him a troubled, hangdog appearance.

Her exhaustion lifted as she greeted the wildly excited dogs, struggling to release them from their pens. The younger of the two, a smooth-haired border collie they called Indie, stood on her back legs and placed her front paws on Lucy's shoulders.

Lucy laughed and pushed her away as the pink tongue missed licking her nose by a whisker. 'Get down, you crazy girl.' She commanded the dog to sit, giggling at the squirming animal trying desperately to obey by keeping her rear end lower than the front, but straining her front half to reach Lucy's hands.

'Come on, Duke. Let me make a fuss of you while this girl practises her manners.' She bent and patted the equally delighted but much more restrained old kelpie, noticing for the first time how grey his muzzle had become.

While Indie gambolled about and Duke trotted sedately to the nearest patch of dry grass to do his business, she filled their water containers and returned to carry the remaining bags from the car.

She dragged them through the kitchen where her father was standing still, gazing through the window. A surge of empathy washed through her as she dumped the bags at the doorway to the hall.

'I'll put the kettle on and find something in the

freezer for dinner,' she said. 'I reckon we both need an early night.'

Rubbing a hand through his thick, brown hair, Brent nodded. 'Sounds good. I'll call the hospital to tell your mother we're home.'

It was barely eight o'clock when Lucy switched off her light. She had opened a blank aerogramme and got as far as writing, *My darling Fergus, I am back on the farm and have so much to tell you.* Then her eyelids had drooped, the pen had wobbled in her loose hand, and she crawled into bed, vowing to rise early and finish it before daylight.

IT DIDN'T HAPPEN and Lucy woke to the sound of the farm ute and barking dogs, the sun already high in the sky. Reassuring herself she would finish her letter later, she struggled out of bed, dressed, swallowed a glass of water, and ate a banana.

Heat hung in the spring air as Lucy backed the tractor out of the shed, a large round bale of hay speared on the front forks. She pressed the lever beside her and the bale rose high, allowing her clear visibility below it.

After confirming plans with her father, Lucy repeated the process of filling each hay rack until every animal had sufficient fodder for the next two days, while Brent drove around each cattle-filled paddock and checked the water troughs.

It was almost midday when Lucy parked the tractor as a familiar white ute pulled up beside the shed. A slim young man stepped out, his eyes shaded by a wide-brimmed hat and his navy-blue shirt sleeves rolled up to the elbow.

'Morning!'

'Hi, Robert.'

He strode over to her and gave her an awkward hug. 'Hi, Cindy.'

They exchanged a smile. As a young boy, he'd struggled to pronounce his "Ls", so he had shortened her full title of "Lucinda"—which only her mother and those who didn't know her well used—to Cindy.

'Sorry to hear about your mum. Sorry too that you had to be called home. Your dad said you were loving Scotland.'

A pang of regret stabbed her, and she nodded. 'Thanks.'

'Your dad around?'

As though on cue, the rattle of the farm ute answered and Brent pulled up beside them.

'How'ya going, Rob?'

'Gidday, Brent. Pretty good, thanks.' He ducked his head. 'Sorry you had to come home to do what I should have done. Our irrigation system broke down and it took us all day to fix it. Planned to nip over first thing this morning but ... you know how it is. Something always happens to hold you up and this morning it was the damn auger—just when we'd only pumped half the grain we needed.'

'All good, mate,' Brent said. 'Cattle weren't making a din, so we knew they weren't starving.'

Robert lifted his hat and rubbed a hand through his sandy hair. 'How's Leigh?'

Brent turned to Lucy. 'Lucy's the expert.'

'Don't know about that, Dad. Thanks for asking though, Robert. At this stage she's comfortable and well cared for. She's being taken to Brisbane on Tuesday for a more detailed scan, so we'll know more after that.' She waved a hand around the yard. 'Meanwhile, we've decided we need to get some cattle work done and take a good look at the crops. There's no rain forecast for a while so it might be worth us making the barley into hay or silage instead of waiting until harvest and finding out the yield cost more than growing it.'

'If you need a hand, I can come over anytime,' Robert said with a longer-than-necessary look at Lucy.

Lucy grinned. 'Unless something else needs your expert attention, you mean?'

'You're right.'

'I reckon Lucy and I'll manage,' Brent said. 'Thanks though. We might need to call on you again during the week, depending on Leigh.'

'No worries.' Robert shot them both a rueful grin and opened the door of his ute, his gaze fixed on Lucy. 'Keep us posted, hey?'

Brent nodded and they waved as he crawled down the drive, a pall of dust trailing in his wake despite his slow speed. He gave a tiny nod. 'He's a good lad. Well, man now I suppose.' He grinned at Lucy. 'Same age as you, isn't he? Another sensible young adult with a good head on his shoulders even though he's the baby of the family.'

While not always generous with compliments, her father's appraisal of both her and Robert should have given her a much-needed boost. But her insides clenched. The look Robert had given her had not only been one of a helpful neighbour. It had been filled with something akin to desire. Intuition flared as she backed away.

'I'm starving, Dad. Let's grab a sandwich. Then we can decide whether we bale the barley or feed it off to the cattle? If it's cutting and baling, I reckon we leave it until next week when we know what Mum's treatment will involve.'

His jaw dropped as he studied Lucy's solemn face. 'You think it's bad, don't you?'

For a long minute, their gazes held. She couldn't lie to him. "Areas of concern" almost always indicated a tumour or growth of some sort, even if the word wasn't spoken until proven true. 'Yeah. I do. But we have to stay positive until we know for certain what is going on. And you know Mum. She'll be lying in that bed now thinking about what needs to be done here—and trusting us to get on with the job.'

Straightening his shoulders, Brent lay an arm over Lucy's. 'Right then, a couple of peanut butter sandwiches, an apple and a cuppa, and we're in business—for your mother's sake.'

As though understanding every word, both dogs bounded ahead of them as Brent opened the house gate, raced to the veranda, and slumped in a heap on either side of the door.

Lucy laughed. 'Like sentries at their post.' She bent and rubbed their ears, then toed off her boots and entered the kitchen.

13

For the next two and a half days, Lucy and her father rose at daylight and worked until dark, pausing only for drink breaks, lunch and a short rest in the heat of the day. Accepting the dusty conditions and the fact the horses hadn't been brushed or ridden in a while, Lucy opted for the quad bike. *Much quicker to jump on and go—we've got a lot to do before Tuesday.*

The cattle were drafted with the enthusiastic assistance of Indie and Duke, and the now well-grown calves locked in the yards with mounds of hay. Lucy and the dogs gathered the cows and, with Lucy idling behind them on the quad and the dogs weaving back and forth, they walked toward the back of the farm where an electric fence had been set up to partition off a third of the struggling barley crop.

Lucy counted them through the gate before closing it, releasing a long, slow breath. It had been a hard decision. Even break feeding, the fact that the dry stalks in this paddock would only last a few days was heartbreaking. But she hoped that by that time, they would have had a chance to cut and bale the rest and then rotate the cows around the stubble before having to distribute any more of the precious lucerne hay. They would save as much of that as they could for Buster, the old bay gelding she'd had for more than ten years, and Goldie, the pretty palomino mare Brent used for campdrafting.

She leaned her head back, shading her eyes with her hand. Not a cloud. No breeze. Just a bright, burning sun in the midst of a vivid blue sky. Her thoughts flashed back to her quiet, melancholy father. He had struggled with agreeing to feed his precious crop to the cattle, and she had needed to coax him into making the decision. He and Leigh had always done things together and now she realised that it had been Leigh, not Brent, who had been the entrepreneurial one in the family.

'Poor Dad,' she whispered. 'You're lost without your mate beside you.' And with a heavy heart, she returned to the yards to check the water.

By Monday evening, the calves had been collected by the carrier and trucked to the Roma Saleyards for the following day's sale and the cows had been moved to stage two of the break-fed paddock, leaving the final third for the couple of days Brent and Lucy would need to be in Toowoomba.

Robert had returned at Brent's request and had promised to feed, water, and run the dogs, and check all stock water and the cows in the back paddock while they were away. Lucy took a long, hard look at the young man opposite her at their kitchen table. He was handsome in a rustic way—not unlike Fergus. Even their eyes were a similar colour. Her stomach did a little skip as a vision of Fergus's face filled her mind, squashing her concerns about Robert. She pushed her chair back and refilled the kettle. Biting back a tear as she waited for it to boil, she stared unseeingly through the window as memories of them walking hand in hand around his green, heather-clad croft flooded her mind.

Turning back to the men at the table, she sighed, wishing with all her being that it was Fergus in Robert's place.

Tonight I will write more to you, my darling—but I will leave enough space to share my mother's results with you tomorrow.

'THE NEUROLOGIST WILL BE ALONG to talk to you all as soon as he's available,' the nurse announced, her face soft but solemn.

For what felt like ages, no one said a word.

'Do you have any idea what the next step will be?' Mandy asked.

'Her scans are being reviewed now. We'll transfer her into another room where a treatment plan will be discussed with you all as soon as possible.'

'How long will she have to stay in hospital?' Brent spoke softly, his eyes damp.

Lucy tucked her arm into his and squeezed it.

'That will depend on what the treatment going forward will be,' the nurse said.

'So, when will we get these answers?' Mandy demanded.

Lucy shot her a frown. 'One step at a time, Mandy. These things can take a while.'

The nurse smiled in acknowledgement. 'Yes, there are a number of consultants in these cases, and it can take time for everyone to be informed. However, we will be progressing your case as speedily as possible.'

'So ... are we talking today? Tomorrow?' Mandy asked in a slightly less aggressive tone.

The nurse took a deep breath. 'I expect we'll know more by late this afternoon. In the meantime, you are welcome to stay with Mrs Pellegreen as long as you like.'

Moments after she left the room, Leigh appeared to gain strength—as though she had been waiting in silence for an answer and now was relieved to know it was close. Her voice was still slurred but clear enough to regain a smidgeon of authority. 'Results have been shared with me, so I suggest that as soon as the team have talked to us all and made their recommendations, you and Dad go home again, Lucy. I know Robert's quite capable, but I'd like to be sure our animals are being cared for the way we do. And Mandy, I don't expect you to hang around here when I know you have a lot to prepare for school.'

Lucy rested her hand on her mother's arm, relieved to hear the thread of positivity in her voice, despite the stressful situation and the knots in her stomach increasing. 'Let's wait until we've spoken with the experts and then we can decide who needs to do what and be where.'

Barely two hours later, Mandy was about to return to the hospital café to fetch their fourth round of coffees for the day when a team of two women and a man entered dressed in white coats.

The man went straight to Leigh's bed and gave her a smile. 'Hello.' He turned to face the family. 'I'm Dr Chris Black, neurosurgeon.' Without preamble, he continued, 'Unfortunately the news is not good. Although Leigh's initial symptoms indicated she may have suffered a stroke, the MRI has revealed a much more serious issue—a brain tumour.'

The family stared at him, stunned.

'B-but,' Mandy began. 'How can that be?'

'It is not uncommon for the first signs of a brain tumour to be similar to those of a stroke. This is why we recommended further investigations.'

One of the women stepped forward. 'I'm Dr Sri Bhattacharya, oncologist,' she indicated the younger woman beside her, 'and this is our oncology registrar, Dr Janet Spencer. We're here to assist with Mrs Pellegreen's treatment.'

Silence filled the room as even Mandy appeared lost for words.

The doctor proceeded to explain that numerous metastases had also been visible in the scan, highlighting the diagnosis of malignant and aggressive cancer.

'We have two choices, Mrs Pellegreen,' Dr Black said, resting on the edge of Leigh's bed and placing a hand on hers. 'We can use radiation and chemo to slow the progress of the tumours—or we can offer you palliative care so you can enjoy time with the family without pain.'

He then suggested that Leigh be discharged. 'You can go home to think about the options and then contact us once you've had time to absorb the situation and have made your decision regarding which treatment you would prefer. I've written a prescription for some steroids which should help the inflammation, in turn, helping your speech. I'd like you to start taking them as soon as possible. The nurse will give you my contact details so you can phone if you have any questions or problems.'

The Pellegreen family gaped at each other in silence before Leigh spoke. 'Thank you, Doctor.' Her voice was barely audible. 'How long have I got?'

He drew a deep breath before answering. 'We never know in these circumstances. It could be weeks or months, but with radiation and chemo, as I said, we hope to slow the progression down and there have been patients who have outlived all expectations.'

'I assume the treatment will make me sick?'

He nodded. 'Unfortunately there are side effects, however we do our best to compensate for them with the use of drugs.'

'Thank you, Doctor. I'll think about it and let you know.'

After expressing their apologies again, the medical team left. Tears streamed down Brent's face, and Mandy began to sob noisily. Lucy bit back the cry she longed to release and hugged her mother tightly, feeling her shake with the effort of controlling her emotions.

'Well. At least we know what's going on—and what's going to happen,' Leigh said. 'I have a "use-by" date stamped on my forehead and I want to go home —now.'

14

———

*A*fter a few minutes, they pulled themselves together and while Mandy and Brent helped pack Leigh's possessions, Lucy hastily scribbled the latest information on the bottom of her aerogramme to Fergus.

'Take my arm, Mum,' Mandy said firmly. 'I'll walk you to the lift and Dad can carry your stuff.'

'I'll get the car and meet you in the pick-up area out the front,' Brent said in a quavering voice.

'And I'll pop downstairs and put this in the post box,' Lucy added. 'See you outside in a few minutes.'

After quickly adding the most tragic news she'd ever had to share—her writing wobbly and erratic—she signed, "with all my love, Lucy." then licked the edges of the paper, folded them over, and pressed them, sealing the letter. Dashing along the corridor, she reached the lift as the doors closed so continued to the stairs and hurried down to the main entrance.

A red post box stood in one corner. Slipping the feather-light blue letter through the slot, she closed her eyes for a moment and conjured the image in her mind—the one she would treasure forever. The one when she first laid eyes on Fergus. The one where a fine, smiling young man followed a flock of sheep up a hill, surrounded by green grass and colourful crocuses dotting the roadside, a black and white dog at his side.

'Are you alright?' a kind voice jolted her back to the present.

Lucy's eyes flew open, and she stared at the woman. Her hair was white and she held an envelope in one hand while the other rested on a walking stick.

'I'm sorry. I was miles away.'

The woman chuckled. 'I could see that. Dreaming of the man you just wrote to?'

Lucy smiled as heat flushed her cheeks. 'Something like that.' Then she lifted her hand in a small wave and darted toward the exit.

IT WAS ALMOST a week before Leigh decided she had to give the treatment a chance. So, having planned to have the initial measuring and face mask made in preparation for the radiation, Brent returned to

Toowoomba with his wife, leaving Lucy in charge of the farm.

'Make sure you phone tonight to let me know how it goes. And if you need me, I'll ring Robert and be there tomorrow,' Lucy said as she waved them goodbye.

School had resumed following the holidays and Mandy announced she was too busy to spend another day at the hospital. Secretly, Lucy was relieved. Her sister's lack of understanding in these situations only complicated the issue—and that was the last thing either of their parents needed.

She spent half an hour brushing the horses while Duke lay in the shade of the tree and Indie sniffed the manure and made two attempts at stealing the curry comb from the grooming box.

'You're a kleptomaniac, Indie.' She snapped off a thick, dead branch from the tree and plonked it on the ground in front of her. 'Here, chew on this while I finish up. Then we've got cattle to feed.'

Glancing at her watch, Lucy threw a freshly washed summer rug on each horse, packed up the kit, and returned it to the shed beside the garage that served the dual purpose of a tack room and storage for the ride-on mower.

With the hay feeders in the cow paddock full again and the troughs functioning satisfactorily, she hurried inside, washed her hands, and glugged down a large glass of cold water.

'Now it's your turn, my darling,' she said aloud as she strode to her bedroom and pulled her writing pad out of her desk drawer. She folded back the cover and removed the well-thumbed blue aerogramme sandwiched between the empty pages, smiling as she reread it for the umpteenth time. Their first letters had crossed and finding Fergus's in the copious mailbox at the foot of their driveway the day after she'd posted hers had lifted her heart beyond belief. She had already written and posted a second—and now she had the house to herself and an hour or two before the mailman was due, she would write another.

She grinned at the large, loopy letters on the flimsy paper—almost as though Fergus had deliberately made the words big so he didn't have to write so many.

Dear Lucy,

You've only been gone two days, but Ardvasar feels empty. I miss you and so does Jet. I swear he's listening out for you because he cocks an ear every time someone walks up the lane.

I hope your mother is alright and treatment has begun. I can't wait until you come home to me again and we can begin our life together.

Meanwhile, I've been keeping myself busy and have started painting the inside of the croft. I found a piece of oak in the shed so will sand it down and dress it then buy a new sink unit. The oak will make a nice kitchen bench. I thought

I'd paint the cupboard doors pale green. What do you think? My dad always said having a deadline is wonderful for getting projects done and as soon as I know when you're coming back, I'll be working overtime to get this wee house perfect for you.

The wind off the sea is freezing today so it's good to be working inside with the fire going. I only wish you were here with me.

I can't think of anything else. Look forward to your letter and reading your news.

All my love,

F xx

She withdrew a new aerogramme from the packet and unfolded it, running a hand over the paper to flatten it. Then she began, her writing as small as she could make it without having Fergus complain he needed a magnifying glass.

With so much to tell him, she began with her love for him and reiterating she missed him as much as he missed her. She detailed the farm's condition, her daily routine of checking water sources, feed, inspecting cattle for buffalo fly, and their frantically busy few days turning half the poorly crops into hay. Their decision to break-feed the other half ensured the cattle had something to graze on, even if it wasn't much, but having to constantly shift the electric fences every second day was a chore as the heat rose and the ground baked into a compacted sheet of brown earth.

The worst part is knowing that without a crop to sell, the farm income will be greatly reduced this year.

It wasn't until the final quarter of the aerogramme that she mentioned her mother—and her current status.

With Mum being terminally ill—she paused and chewed the end of the pen as the now familiar ache of disbelief and sorrow crept over her, shrouding her in panic and hopelessness—*I don't know what I should do. I haven't mentioned our upcoming wedding. Everyone has been so worried, and I'd feel bad talking about us and our happiness while Mum is sick. Her future doesn't look bright but I'm hoping the radiation and chemo will get her into remission. When that happens, I'll tell both Mum and Dad about our wedding and hope she'll be well enough to travel to Scotland for it. Dad has taken her to Toowoomba today for the preparation part of the radiation and then she will begin treatment tomorrow. He will stay with her for the two weeks of radiation, then the chemo begins. I guess we'll be told more about that stage when it draws closer.*

Meanwhile, my love, the mailman will be at the gate soon and I want him to collect this letter. Maybe he will have another one from you for me? It's frustrating only having two deliveries each week but I suppose that's country life for you.

Lots of love, Lucy xxxxxxxxx

She quickly re-read the letter then sealed it and glanced at her watch again. It was almost midday. The dusty silver four-wheel drive usually pulled up at their gate between twelve-thirty and one o'clock, so she had plenty of time. Nevertheless, she would hate to miss Merv's cheery smile and efficient exchange of goodies, so she dashed to the veranda and grabbed her hat before shoving her feet into well-worn riding boots and marching down the long driveway with the dogs at her heels.

LATER THAT NIGHT, she wasn't sure how long she had been asleep on the couch, waiting for her father's call, when the barking of dogs woke her. Throwing back the light rug she'd pulled over herself, she stumbled sleepily toward the back door.

Flicking on the lights, her thundering heart quickened as the outdoor floodlight shone on her parents.

'Is everything alright?'

'Tell you in a minute,' her father said wearily. 'Put the kettle on would you, love?'

Slumped in the kitchen chair, Leigh met her daughter's gaze. Her face was ashen with exhaustion, contrasting with her thick, brown hair with its copper lights and not a hint of grey in it. 'I couldn't do it.'

Lucy turned to her father, brows raised.

He shook his head and shrugged.

'It was that cage thing they put on your head—and

that awful tunnel machine. It was all too much and I knew there was no way I could be in there for a second. I'd rather accept my lot and stay here where I'm happy. The palliative care team have discussed my case with the Roma hospital, and I've got a heap of medications to keep me pain-free.'

For a few seconds, Lucy clamped her lips together, biting back hot, frustrated, heartbroken tears as she hugged her mother. But they refused to be contained, bursting out and saturating her mother's shoulder. 'I'm sorry, so, so sorry,' she sobbed.

'We all are,' Brent said quietly as he placed three steaming mugs of tea on the table. 'But this is your mother's choice.'

Lucy sniffed, fished in her dressing gown pocket for a tissue, and blew her nose. 'I know.' She drew a deep shuddering breath and squared her shoulders. 'I'm here for you, Mum. I'll be able to nurse you.'

'Thank you, dear.' Leigh's voice was clearer now, the steroids having settled whatever was affecting her speech.

Lucy hoped they would help stem the aggressiveness of the tumours' growth, even for a short while.

It was after midnight before they all went to bed. Lucy lay staring through the bedroom window, focusing on the stars that shone in the inky night. While the family had not been regular church-goers, it was not the first time Lucy had prayed. Now silent words filled her head as she sent her deepest wishes into the aether. After asking for her mother's reprieve, she added, *I take that back. I know the horrible disease will win, but please, please keep her pain free and able to think of all the wonderful things she's done in her life.*

She longed to be able to phone Fergus and share her sorrow, her hurt, and her love ... but an international call was hideously expensive—and from that moment on, she was shackled to the farm if not the house for the foreseeable future. Any hope of returning to Scotland in the next few months was gone.

But Mum must come first. Despite convincing herself, a dull, desperate ache sat like lead in the bottom of her stomach.

Early dawn spread purple rays over the dusty paddocks as Lucy eventually dropped into a deep, exhausted sleep.

15

Queensland, June 2024 – Ingrid

OVER TWO WEEKS passed before Ingrid found time to open her laptop and log on. Her father was to be moved to a sunny, friendly, and caring nursing home within the next few days and although Vonnie had shed buckets of tears, she accepted her beloved Tony, husband of forty years, was no longer the man she married and needed care she was unable to provide.

Ingrid's return to work had begun as exhausting as she remembered. No change there. She almost galloped across the room to answer a patient's call. The pace was always frantic in the emergency department, but at least it was varied. While she tended to patients and completed the never-ending mountain of paperwork, her mind occasionally flew to Callum and a nervous anxiety gnawed at her stomach.

I have to find time to write to him—tonight.

And so, after preparing dinner while her mother laboriously showered Tony, insisting she preferred to do it alone, Ingrid slid her laptop to the corner of the kitchen bench and trawled through social media, searching for the name "Pellegreen". One came from Canada—a young man with a mop of curly hair and a set of skis tucked under his arm. Another teenager living in Minnesota popped up. There were a few more but none that fitted the age bracket Lucy would be in.

'You can put the fish on to cook now, dear,' Vonnie said, casting a glance toward the laptop as Ingrid closed it. 'Your father's ready to eat.'

While busying herself with the meal, Ingrid frowned as she searched for ideas of where to begin.

'Is something bothering you?' Vonnie asked.

Ingrid shook her head. 'Not really.' Her mother's question came as a surprise. Ingrid hadn't mentioned Callum or the quest the two of them had challenged themselves to. Vonnie had enough on her mind without Ingrid loading her with anything else. Her days were already consumed with worry and angst.

'We'll talk later,' Vonnie said firmly.

Expecting her mother to forget and fall into bed beside her husband early as she did every other night,

Ingrid was surprised when Vonnie returned to the kitchen after settling Tony.

'Something is worrying you—and it's not only your father.'

Ingrid sighed, gave the bench a final wipe, and faced her mother. 'Alright then. I haven't mentioned anything because I decided you were busy enough. But ... you know I had a lovely holiday, especially on the Isle of Skye.'

Vonnie raised her eyebrows and smiled, easing the lines that had formed on her face. 'And?'

'Long story short. I met a man—an older man, probably around your age. He came into the hotel where I was staying, and we met again while I was out walking. Anyway, he invited me for a cup of tea. And ... before you say anything, his nephew, Callum, was also there. Callum showed me around Skye for a couple of days and we are staying in contact—not that I've had a chance to do any more than exchange a few texts.' She paused, a grin hovering on her lips as her mother leaned forward, her eyes brighter than they'd been since Ingrid got home. 'It turns out that this older man, Fergus, had an Australian friend—whom Callum and I believe was his girlfriend. He had a pile of aerogrammes he showed us.'

Vonnie rubbed her hands together. 'Ooh, this sounds interesting.'

'Apparently the girl he was exchanging letters with

just stopped writing. He couldn't find out why and has been a bit sad ever since, I think. He certainly seemed it anyway—and he has never married or had a girl-friend as far as Callum knows.'

'So you and Callum have decided to collude and see if you can find this woman?'

Ingrid chuckled. Her mother was as romantic as she was. *Perhaps her assistance is just what she needs to help distract her from Dad's problems?*

'Yes. I've had a look through social media with no luck. The trouble is, her surname was Pellegreen but if she married, it's probably changed, and I haven't a clue where to begin to find her.' She shrugged, lifting upturned hands as she spoke.

'Do you know where she was living?'

'Apparently out on a property somewhere west of Roma.'

'Well. That's only about a four-hour drive away. You never know. The post office may be able to help. Oh, and the electoral roll too. I believe you can look it up if you have a name.'

Buoyed with renewed enthusiasm—and surprise at her mother's interest—Ingrid jumped up and hugged her. 'You're a treasure. Once we get Dad settled into the nursing home, we could go on a road trip to Roma?'

Vonnie shook her head. 'It would be nice. But I won't be going anywhere for a while. Your father's my priority and I want to spend every minute I can with him. None of us know how long we've got, and he's been my best friend for over forty years.'

A lump caught in the back of Ingrid's throat at her mother's matter-of-fact statement. A sudden, stabbing pain ran through her and she wished she could take back her flippant suggestion. Of course Vonnie wouldn't leave Tony as long as he was alive. She would simply transfer her daily attention from caring for him at home to visiting the new residence and sitting with him for as long as the staff allowed.

'Okay. I'll look up the electoral roll and on my next break of at least two days, I'll nip out to Roma, visit the post office, and maybe ask around the pubs and shops. It would be easier if we didn't have so many privacy laws these days,' she groaned.

Vonnie grimaced. 'If we didn't have them, just imagine how many more problems we'd have in society. Armed break-ins and abused women—and men. Things are bad enough now but without those laws, anyone would be able to stalk ex-partners and such like.' She shook her head and shuddered. 'No, best that things are kept as secure as possible—even if it is painful when you're trying to do a genuine search like this.'

'Thanks, Mum. You've been a great help. I'll email Callum and let him know I'm making a start.'

They shared a hug and Vonnie meandered down

the hallway toward the bedrooms while Ingrid flipped open the laptop and began.

An hour later, after trawling through the electoral roll and finding no-one with the surname of Pellegreen listed in the Maranoa electorate, Ingrid expanded the search into the connecting electorates and eventually gave up.

'Right then. Next step is to check my roster and then book a motel in Roma for a night,' she whispered.

Clicking into her emails, she entered Callum's address and commenced writing.

Hi there!

Sorry about the delay in getting this written. It's been a bit chaotic here with all the business for Dad, and it took me a few days to recover from jet lag this time. I wonder why it didn't happen when I went from "Down Under" to the northern hemisphere?

Thanks for your text asking how my father was. It's not good news but we have found a nursing home for him, so next week we'll move him in and hopefully that will give Mum a break. She will still go and sit with him every day —but I don't blame her. They've been together for yonks and I reckon it'll take her a while to adjust.

Anyway. How are you? I guess summer would be in full swing now and the tourists clogging the streets of Skye. I hope you got all the sheep shorn and they're now skipping around naked on the common for the warmer months.

Winter has arrived here and although it hasn't got too

cold yet, the leaves are piled up down the roadsides and I've added a warmer doona to my bed.

Now for the search report (or lack of!). No luck tracking a Lucy Pellegreen—or any Pellegreen for that matter. That's not quite true. There are a few on Facebook and Instagram but none that fit Lucy's profile, and anyway, I suspect that if she's still alive, she is married and under a different name. Then I moved on to the electoral roll but once again, no luck. I have a couple of days off coming up so thought I'd take a drive out to Roma for a night and see what I can find. Maybe the post office, pubs or shops might remember someone of that name. It's been a joke here in Australia that people in country areas remember everyone and everything that happened for generations. Let's hope that's the case this time! I'll keep you posted (by email and text of course, not by blue-aerogramme-snail-mail).

Look forward to hearing from you.

She paused, considering how she should sign off. An emoji? Love from ...? In the end, she simply signed,

Ingrid xx

16

---

*L*ess than a week later, she was strolling along McDowall Street in Roma, heading for the post office. A cool breeze lifted her hair. She paused to search her bag for a hair tie then turned her face into the breeze and fastened the long, blonde strands in a ponytail.

Her heart pounded as she walked up the steps and entered the brick-clad building. There were two staff serving at their respective alcoves, one a stern-looking middle-aged woman and the other a young, pimply-faced lad. She stood back for a moment, hesitating before joining the queue. Neither looked as though they would be particularly helpful, although she wasn't sure why she made that assumption. Drawing a deep breath, she waited, hoping she would be called to the young guy, but knowing the older woman would probably know more about the district—and the past.

'Next please,' the woman called.

Ingrid clutched her bag against her and strode to the counter.

'How can I help?' The woman smiled, the expression completely changing her demeanour.

Ingrid returned the smile, stuttering out her words with relief. 'I-I'm hoping you might be able to help me?'

The woman raised one eyebrow. 'I'll try,' she said.

'I'm looking for someone. A person who lived on a property west of here over thirty years ago.'

The woman's head tilted to one side as she leaned on the counter. 'Not sure anyone here can help you. None of us worked here that far back.' She nodded toward the young fellow. 'He's just out of school and I only moved here a few years ago. Even if we did remember this ... "person", there's been a lot of changes in the district. What property did this "person" live on?'

In an instant, Ingrid realised the woman's interest had changed from one of potential helpfulness to nosiness as her eyes flickered with what could only be interpreted as excitement.

'Binnalong,' Ingrid said quietly.

The woman drew back, her eyes narrowing before she shook her head.

'Nope. Never heard of that one—least not around here anyway. There's plenty of properties called Binnalong but none on our mail runs.'

Ingrid stepped away from the counter. 'Okay. Thanks anyway.'

Back on the footpath, Ingrid paused and looked in all directions. Her stomach rumbled as she spotted a pub on the corner a block away. *Perhaps someone there will be able to help—and I can have lunch at the same time.*

While she ploughed her way through the most enormous chicken schnitzel she'd ever been served, she studied those around her. A party of twelve people filled one end of the dining area, their raucous laughter and conversations overpowering the television set above them. Several couples sat at smaller tables, while two groups with young children had an area that appeared almost designated to them. She blinked at the mess the children were making. *Good idea.*

'Everything alright?' a bright young voice beside her made her jump. She hadn't seen her coming. *What's happened to my brilliant observation skills?*

'Yes. Thanks. All good.'

The girl wiped the table next to Ingrid, her enthusiasm brisk and efficient. She hummed while she worked.

'Um. Excuse me,' Ingrid said. 'Are you a local?'

The girl paused and grinned. 'Sure am. Well, sort of, anyway.'

Ingrid hesitated. What did 'sort of' mean?

'Why do you want to know?'

'I'm looking for someone. Well, a property actually. Apparently it used to be on Roma's mail run but no-one at the post office was able to help me.'

'Oh? What's its name?'

'Binnalong.'

She frowned, her head tilted to one side. 'That rings a bell.'

Ingrid straightened as her heart leapt in hope.

'I think I've heard it mentioned somewhere.'

Ingrid held her breath, waiting for a positive answer.

The young girl shook her head. 'Sorry. It's familiar but I can't place it.' She shot Ingrid an apologetic smile and pointed to the meal in front of her. 'Better get that down you before it goes cold.'

Ingrid sat for another fifteen minutes, sipping her coffee and picking at her meal. Then, unable to finish, she rose, picked up her bag, and headed for the restrooms.

Minutes later, Ingrid was about to open the door to the footpath when the slim, young girl called out to her. 'Hey. Lady. Wait a bit.'

Ingrid stopped, blinking at the pretty, animated face while a solid, bald-headed man reached past her and wrenched open the door, knocking Ingrid against the waitress.

'Oi. Watch whatcha doing, Pauly,' the waitress said.

'Sorry.' He grinned apologetically at them both and continued on his way.

Ingrid ignored the man, focusing on the young girl as a tiny bit of hope lifted her despondency.

'I just remembered where I've heard the Binnalong name. It was at a party I went to recently with my boyfriend. Near my aunty and uncle's place half an hour west of here. They were talking about some big landholder. They called the property Dalgonally but I think a piece of it used to be called Binnalong. All gone now apparently—amalgamated into the "empire".' She made quotation marks with her fingers in the air, a lopsided grin on her face as though not impressed by the territory claimed.

'Oh, that's great. Thank you. What happened to the family who owned Binnalong?'

She shrugged. 'No idea. I guess they died. Or sold out. Otherwise, why would the property name have been changed?'

Ingrid thanked her and stepped out into the surprisingly warm air. She dawdled back to the motel, her shoulders alternately drooping and rising again as her hopes roller-coasted with every step.

Why indeed? I've got the property name, so it's worth a try.

BACK IN HER ROOM, Ingrid checked the internet for the name "Dalgonally", delighted to discover a fancy website advertising stud cattle and listing the address of the property. She studied the app on her phone. *On the highway—and less than an hour away?* She couldn't believe her luck. After checking the time, she scrambled off the bed, snatched up her bag, and slammed the door behind her as she hurried to her car.

"In two hundred metres, you will reach your destination," the navigation system announced. Ingrid breathed a sigh of relief. The distance had been greater than she had expected, and she hadn't had time to enjoy the scenery. Focusing on avoiding the massive road trains wanting to overtake her little car, and the caravanners tootling along at ten to twenty kilometres below the speed limit, took all her concentration.

Peering through the windscreen, her hand held across her forehead to shade the glare, she followed the tinny sound, "You have reached your destination," and shuddered over the wide cattle grid beside a massive sign for Dalgonally. Fifty metres into the property, a series of signposts greeted her, offering a multitude of options. *Yards, Dalgonally One, Dalgonally Two, and Dalgonally Three.* There were more, some listing bore numbers, but none of them made any sense to her. 'Good grief,' she muttered. 'Anyone would think we're in Piccadilly Circus.'

Uncertain of which way she should go, she decided on Dalgonally One. It sounded the most important so she hoped at least someone would be able to help her. The track was lightly gravelled and relatively smooth, however she slowed to a crawl, anxious to avoid the potholes that seem to appear from nowhere.

A large, timber homestead came into view, surrounded by lush green lawns, shrubs, and a few shady trees. On the opposite side of the huge expanse of bare earth that appeared to serve as an intersection was a massive shed with two smaller buildings beyond it. *Workers cottages?* She drew up beside a huge, ancient bottle tree in the centre of the yard as a young woman emerged from one of the smaller buildings.

Ingrid got out of the car and waited as the girl walked toward her.

'Hi there. Can I help you?'

Ingrid swallowed, her pulse pounding with anticipation. 'Hello. I'm looking for someone.'

The girl seemed surprised. 'Who?'

'A woman by the name of Lucy. Lucy Pellegreen.'

The girl's face screwed into an apologetic frown and she shook her head. 'Sorry. I've only been here a few days. I'm the new governess. There's a few of us here but no-one called Lucy, and I've never heard the name Pellegreen.' She paused for a moment and narrowed her eyes as though it hurt to think. 'There's Kelly, Mara, Felicity and Rachael here. They're out mustering cattle at the moment. There's a few blokes around too—and the owners of course. It's a big place so there's lots of staff, even if most of its only seasonal.' She drew a deep breath. 'But I'm sorry. As I said, no-one called Lucy.'

'Would anyone else know?' Ingrid glanced around, a little surprised at the lack of action. She had expected a property this big would have had more evidence of its workforce.

'Maybe. Only, I'm on my own here at the moment. The cattle work needs everyone available ... apparently. And the boss's wife's gone to Brisbane to help their daughter pack up and move home. That's why I've been employed. Apparently her husband's shot through and left her with three kids. She's some kind of journalist and will be working from here—so I'll be looking after the children.'

Ingrid's eyebrows raised a notch. *I'm not sure you should be telling me all this.* 'What about older women? Perhaps around middle age?' Ingrid persisted hopefully.

'There's the boss's wife, Kylie—and the cook. But she's gone to town to pick up groceries. Like I said, I've only been here a short while and I haven't met a Lucy.'

'Have you heard of a farm called Binnalong?'

The girl shook her head. 'Nah. Sorry. Can't help there either.'

A sting of hopelessness pierced Ingrid. She stared into the girl's face, reassuring herself that she wasn't hiding anything. 'Okay. Thanks very much. Perhaps I've come to the wrong place.'

'Yeah. I know how you feel. It's easy to get lost out here. Long roads leading all over the place but not a lot of people to ask.' The girl softened, her sympathy genuine.

Ingrid glanced westward, surprised to notice dark clouds drawing closer. A shadow passed overhead, and she gave an involuntary shudder.

'I'd better get back to town. Thanks for your help.'

The girl remained where she was while Ingrid turned the car and waved goodbye.

$\mathcal{B}$ack on the highway, Ingrid was relieved the traffic had lessened, so she set the cruise control to a hundred and consoled herself by taking notice of the scenery as she travelled. Houses were few and far between, set well off the road, their positions only obvious by the clumps of trees and shrubs surrounding them. Paddocks were massive, a few drier expanses dotted with eucalypts and cattle, with the rest, a rich green swathe of healthy, growing crops.

'Sorry, Callum. Not much to tell you tonight,' she muttered. Nevertheless, her disappointment faded a little at the thought of talking to him.

She glanced in the rear-vision mirror. The black clouds appeared to be following her much more quickly than she'd expected. Notching her cruise control up a few clicks, she focused on the road ahead, hoping there were no traffic patrols in the area as the telephone poles sped by.

Thunder cracked seconds after she reached the motel, followed by loud, fat drops of rain. Then, before she had locked the car and closed her unit door, the skies opened and the water teamed down in sheets.

Thankful she was still too full of lunch to bother with any dinner, she boiled the kettle and made herself a cup of tea then removed the tub of yogurt from the tiny fridge and sat on her bed. It was still early morning on the Isle of Skye—too early to ring Callum yet.

Instead she checked the time—almost five o'clock —and rang her mother, confident she would still be at the nursing home and wouldn't be busy. Vonnie's routine had become a repetitive round of rising early, heading off for a walk (which Ingrid had encouraged), then spending an hour or two catching up with house-work and washing before she prepared for the day with her husband. After she'd helped him with his evening meal—regularly served at five-thirty, she would walk with him back to his room and help him get into bed. They knew the carers would perform these tasks, but Vonnie clutched desperately to the hope Tony's condition would stabilise. The last thing she wanted was to lose him. As though giving him every minute of her day would prevent that from happening, she vowed to continue.

'How's Dad?' Ingrid asked as chirpily as she could manage.

'Not so good today. No point in talking to him as he's struggling to recognise anyone.'

Ingrid could feel the devastation in her mother's voice. Her stomach sank.

'How did you get on with your search?' Vonnie asked, her tone brighter now.

Ingrid blew out a breath. 'I'm disappointed.' She relayed the events of the day, hoping her mother would suggest something she hadn't already thought of but she didn't. They chatted companionably for a few more minutes before saying goodbye and ending the call.

Glancing at her watch, Ingrid swiped to her recent calls and tapped Callum's name.

'Good morning!' he answered cheerily.

'Hi there. You're awake then?'

'Sure am. Sun's high in the sky already and I'm stoking my body with coffee before heading off to Fergus's croft.'

He sounded so chipper Ingrid was almost reluctant to share her bad news. She lay back wearily, thankful she hadn't attempted a video call. An image of his twinkling blue eyes and wide grin flashed through her memory as she glanced down at her crumpled shirt.

She pulled the hair tie out of her ponytail and ran her fingers through the knotted strands that splayed over the pillow.

'Sounds fabulous. Sheep work again?'

He snorted a laugh. 'Nope. Today I'm spreading fertiliser on the paddocks. Fergus's wee croft first then I'll do ours here. M'dad phoned last night. He's panicking about all that needs doing—doesn't think I'll manage without him. Between us all—that's me, Fergus, and Mum, we've convinced him to stay put for another few weeks and make the most of a rest. But ... you know how stubborn we Scots cannae be.' He laughed then and she couldn't help but smile at the reference she'd heard many times from her grandmother.

'Anyway, enough about me. Any luck today?'

She heaved an audible sigh. 'Unfortunately not. No leads from the post office. But I did locate a property a girl in the pub put me on to, Dalgonally. It was supposedly once connected to Binnalong. Then I spent two hours driving out there and back. The only person around was the governess—and she was about as useful as a cat flap on a submarine. However, she did confirm there was no property around there called Binnalong.' She paused. 'Do you think the address on the aerogrammes was false?'

'I doubt it. If the address was wrong, the letters wouldn't have reached Lucy to answer them. From the way Fergus talked about her, I could tell he was smitten and the letters were spread over a few weeks so they would have to be genuine.'

'Good point. Sorry, that was a stupid thought. So … back to the drawing board.'

'Hey. Don't worry.' At his caring, sympathetic tone, a wave of calm encircled her. 'We haven't lost any more than we started with—and we've gained a lot, especially our friendship.'

INGRID WOKE with renewed determination the following morning. Talking to Callum had smoothed her disappointment and, although she had to return home in time to work a late shift at the hospital, she decided she would try one more time and visit the post office. It was really their only hope of establishing the existence of "Binnalong" and perhaps, a family by the name of Pellegreen.

While the now familiar young lad served a customer, there was no sign of the older woman. Ingrid dithered, considering leaving again when a middle-aged man appeared from somewhere out the back and placed a parcel on the counter.

'There you go. I hope it's filled with treasure for you.'

The lady he spoke to laughed and thanked him

before turning away and stuffing the parcel into an enormous carry bag.

'Can I help you, love?' the man said.

Ingrid glanced behind her. She was the only customer, so she straightened her shoulders and stepped forward. 'I popped in here yesterday but unfortunately, no one could help me. Perhaps you could?'

'I'm sure I can,' he said jovially, his nose beaming red in the weathered face.

'I'm looking for someone—or a property really. Only, the last confirmation of the address was thirty-four years ago.'

The man guffawed. 'Huh! I have trouble remembering what I did yesterday,' he said.

Her shoulders sagged.

'But I'll try,' he added.

'I'm looking for a woman who lived on a property called "Binnalong". Her name was Lucy Pellegreen.'

He screwed up his face as though the effort of thinking was excruciatingly painful. Then he rubbed his chin with his thumb and forefinger and took a deep, noisy breath. 'Jeez, that's a hard one. I've been here nearly fifteen years but, in that time, I can't honestly say I've heard of either the property or the woman's name. No Pellegreens on our mail service runs to my knowledge. Trouble is, we don't even keep records that far back now so I can't really help you.'

'I see.' Ingrid shrugged. 'Never mind. Thanks anyway.'

'Sorry, love.'

She turned to leave then stopped. 'What is the situation with mail runs now? Are property names still used, or are all addresses a numbered system?'

'They're numbered—using the distance from the beginning of the road to their mailbox. Lots of people still write the property name too, but there's plenty who don't. I guess the older generation are not writing like they used to. Phone's much easier—and cheaper these days—and except for bills, most of what gets delivered are packages and parts for farm equipment.'

'I guess so. Thanks anyway.'

'You could leave your name and phone number if you like. I'm only here a couple of days a week but I can ask around for you and if I hear anything, I'll give you a cooee, hey?'

She shot him a smile. 'That would be great.' After scribbling her details and Lucy's name and address on a piece of notepaper, she thanked the man again and left.

As she made her way back to the motel, she stopped and entered the most established-looking shops and asked the staff the now repetitive question. Again, she was met by blank looks or nosey questioning that clearly had nothing to do with either Binnalong or Lucy Pellegreen. Returning to the motel, she gathered her gear, checked out, and drove slowly to the highway. Then, planting her foot on the accelerator, she sighed. *Not exactly what I had hoped, but at least it's something—and more positive than yesterday.*

Thinking about their lengthy phone call the previous evening, her heart lifted as a vision of Callum's gentle smile sprang into her mind. She flicked the radio to media. Another romantic audiobook was just what she needed as she made her way back to Toowoomba.

Perhaps her father would be having a good day? Reality slammed into her, and she sighed again. Those days were gone. Now the only positive of his horrible, heartbreaking illness was that it was unlikely he would linger long.

Pushing the thought to the back of her mind, Ingrid concentrated on the building relationship between a reclusive middle-aged man and a vibrant, artistic woman emerging from her sound system, the warmth of a loving relationship wrapping around her.

Not unlike Fergus and Lucy really. But hopefully without a disastrous outcome. Had theirs been a tragic ending? She shuddered at the thought.

Shuffling in her seat, she sat taller, her jaw set. *Don't worry, Fergus. I WILL find out what happened to Lucy.*

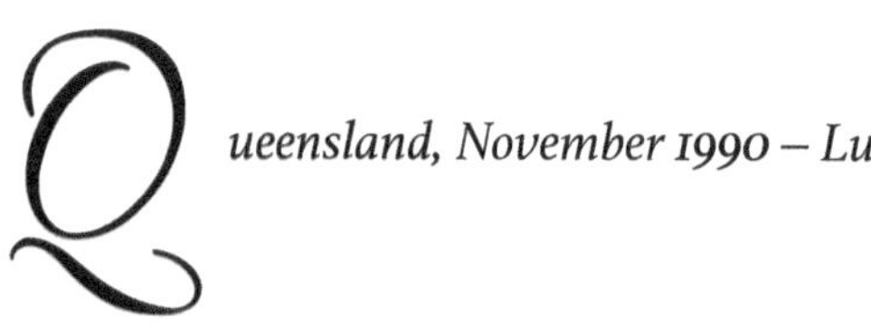

18

Queensland, November 1990 – Lucy

THE WEEKS FLEW by as the drought continued, the days progressively growing hotter than the one before while Lucy's time on the farm became more hectic than ever.

Although steroids had helped Leigh through her first three weeks at home, she refused to admit she was beaten. District nurses visited daily, relieving either Lucy or her father to complete farm chores until almost seven weeks after her diagnosis, Leigh whispered goodbye and succumbed to the illness.

The following days were a whirl of visitors, funeral plans, and tears. Mandy came home briefly, and although both Lucy and Brent were grateful for her well-practiced management skills, they also breathed a relieved sigh when she returned to Brisbane.

Fergus had been vigilant in his letter-writing. Every Friday, the bundle in the mailbox contained a pale blue letter which Lucy excitedly removed. She read the letters several times, breathing in the memories and taking her mind back to Skye as she continued with feeding stock, checking water troughs, and maintaining both the house and garden. Following Leigh's death, Brent spent almost all his time in the shed. His excuse was that the machinery needed servicing and until they got rain, the drought provided the perfect opportunity.

But Lucy knew it was more than that. Brent and Leigh had never known any other relationship, and the emptiness Lucy understood her father to be suffering was unmistakable. Each evening, he stumbled into the laundry, scrubbed his greasy hands and arms, and sat at the kitchen table, his thin face sagging into wrinkles, depicting a much older man than his years.

Lucy was desperate to return to Skye but there was no way she could leave her father or return to nursing —even if she'd wanted to. Her only hope was that Brent's grief would ease soon and, although life would never be the same, at least she would be free to continue with her own plans.

Summer arrived early to inland Queensland and the temperatures soared. The cattle became lethargic, munching on rationed quantities of hay and grain under the hot sun. Lucy sympathised. Perspiration trickled down her back, soaking her cotton shirt while her hair became a sticky mess under her wide-brimmed Akubra.

After dinner on Sunday nights, she wrote to Fergus, detailing the week's work, her father's state of mind—and her love and desperation to return to Skye.

On the first Monday morning in November, Lucy dropped her letter to Fergus in the empty drum and propped up the flag to indicate there was mail to be collected. Returning to the homestead, she glanced across the front paddock opposite where the horses currently stood under a tree, swishing their tails listlessly. Squinting, she focused on a loose wire before slowly shifting her gaze to the entire fence line. She switched off the quad bike and strode across the hard-baked earth.

Groaning after her inspection, she returned to the machinery shed and called her father several times, eventually locating him lying on his back underneath the hay baler.

'Dad. Termites have got into the fence posts in the front paddock. I reckon we should replace it now. Easier to get the job done in good weather, even if the ground is hard.'

He grunted and slid himself into the open before

standing. 'Yeah. I noticed that before you came home —before your mum ...'

'You didn't spray the termites?'

He shook his head. 'Forgot. We've got plenty of time. Doesn't look like the drought's going to break any time soon.'

A surge of exasperation flashed through her for a second. Brent had hammered the old-fashioned saying of "A stitch in time saves nine" into her as she was growing up. But it had been a horrible few months for him and forgetting jobs that needed doing had become commonplace.

Taking a deep breath, she lay a gentle hand on his arm. 'Let's get into it first thing in the morning. While the cattle are in the back paddocks, we can pull the posts out and burn them. I'll ring and order steel replacements and perhaps we could get the job done before rain arrives,' she finished with a half-hearted laugh as they both tilted their heads to stare hopefully at a clear blue sky.

'That's my girl.' He drew himself up and faced her. 'I don't suppose your mum would be happy if she thought we were letting the place fall into rack and ruin.'

She nodded. 'You're right. So, tomorrow we start. Should we ask Robert if he's free to give us a hand?'

'Yes. We'll order posts then get the old fence down. Then perhaps he could come and help us put them in.'

'Perfect.' She stepped forward and hugged him quickly. 'I've got the sprinklers running on the garden, so I'll nip over and turn them off. Then we'll have lunch. Okay?'

He returned her smile. 'Okay.'

REMOVING the rotten posts using the tractor and strong, steel cable was the easy part. While Lucy dragged each one into a pile, Brent wound any reusable wire onto reels.

'I'll run the bucket over the ground, Dad. Smooth it out so we've got a clean slate to use for the new fence.' For the first time in her life, it had been Lucy instructing and encouraging her father, instead of the other way around. His mind seemed to be everywhere but on the project at hand, despite his agreement. Lucy frowned. It had been bad enough caring for her mother, but she had never considered her father would need just as much care—even if it was in a different way.

Relieved that Robert had seemed enthusiastic about helping with the new fence, Lucy sent her father out to check the troughs while she worked until dark. The tinder-dry pile of posts caught alight instantly, and she breathed a sigh of relief it was a still, calm evening.

Ensuring the fire was down to embers and was no

risk to the few remaining blades of dry, dead grass in the paddock, Lucy raked them into a heap and climbed back onto the tractor.

The new steel posts had arrived that afternoon.

'Must be short of work,' her father had said.

After switching the forks for the bucket and running a smooth surface along the soon-to-be new fence line, Lucy exchanged the equipment again. With a tiny window of daylight left, she would shift the new posts into place, saving precious time the following day. Decision made, Lucy thrust the gearstick into reverse, reminding herself that creating something new was always rewarding. She sang as she worked.

Sliding the tractor's dual forks under the tightly packed bundle of posts, she rolled them on, alternating between guiding the front-end loader poles from the tractor seat and grunting with effort as she physically lined them up. Eventually she had the pack neatly wrapped in cable, the sturdy metal hook clipped around the wire to secure them to the forks.

Slowly and carefully, she chugged to the paddock and lowered the posts to the ground.

Even with thick, leather gloves on her hands, untying the cable was more difficult than she expected.

At last, the hook flew free as she bent to roll the posts away. At that exact moment, a vehicle, its head-lights shining, drove along the track toward her. She glanced up at it, unaware of the hook swinging as though celebrating its freedom. Nor did she hear the clank as it hit the tractor and bounced into the air.

With her focus on the approaching vehicle, she didn't see the heavy chunk of steel swing toward her and when it connected with her head, the last she knew was her world turning black.

19

———

The low hum of voices reached her first. Her lashes fluttered frantically as she struggled to open her eyes. Was there something sitting on them? It certainly felt like it, but she persisted, wishing she hadn't the second glaring light blurred her vision.

Taking a breath, she turned her head, blinking in an attempt to clear the mist.

'It's alright, Lucy. Take your time and don't panic.' The voice was unfamiliar, a gentle but firm woman's tone.

She licked her lips, coughing as she attempted to speak. 'Where am I?'

'You're in hospital. Had a nasty disagreement with a steel hook from what I've been told.'

She closed her eyes again and screwed up her forehead as she searched her memory. Nothing. The nurse had called her Lucy. Was that her name?

A hand rested on her arm. 'Everything's okay. You've been in an induced coma for a couple of days. We're letting you wake up now.'

While the words vaguely registered, the reasoning behind it was too much. She closed her eyes again, searching for oblivion.

UNSURE WHAT DAY it was but believing at least one more had passed since she first awoke, she was propped in a seating position when a white-coated man and a woman in pretty blue-patterned clothes joined her. After a brief exchange of greeting, the man explained they were here to check on her and almost immediately flashed a torch in her eyes. The woman stood beside her bed, a clipboard in her hand.

'Lucinda,' the man began. 'Or do you prefer Lucy?'

She stared at him. How did she know? She didn't even know what her name was until the staff had called her Lucy. 'Either,' she said, deciding it was easier.

'You've had a nasty bang on the head. The swelling has reduced—which is a good thing—so we'd like to ask you a few questions if that's alright.'

'I guess so. My head feels like someone's tried to squash it in a vice.'

'I know,' the man continued. 'I'm your doctor—Stephen May. We'll be keeping you on medication for a while until you feel better. Do you remember anything about the accident?'

She squeezed her eyelids together and tried to remember. Her name was Lucinda. She got that. But Lucinda who?

'No,' she whispered.

'What about your home? Do you know where you live?'

Panic surged inside her, heat rising through her body. Was this a test? If she got the questions wrong, what would happen?

Shaking her head gently, she lifted her hand and swiped the tear that trickled over her cheek.

'That's okay. Don't stress. It's early days. Memory loss is common after head injuries. You were very lucky. Had the impact been in a different spot, the outcome could have been ... well, not good.' His smile was gentle and encouraging. 'It will require time, but we'll take things slowly and I'm sure everything will gradually come back to you.'

He rested a light hand briefly on her arm. 'I'll be back later to see how you're feeling.'

As he left the room, the nurse straightened her pillow and smoothed the bedcover.

'Your dad has been coming in each day—and your boyfriend arrived last night too. You gave them a big fright. We phoned your father to let him know you're conscious and he said he'll pop in to see you later.' She smiled then glanced toward the door as a trolley operated by a woman in a taupe-coloured uniform stopped in the corridor.

'How's the patient today?' the woman asked. 'I believe you're ready to eat so that's a good start.'

With the nurse's help, a narrow table was wheeled over her bed and a tray placed on it containing a covered bowl, a glass, and a small plastic container of juice.

'Shall I help you sit up more?' the nurse asked.

She shook her head then wished she hadn't. Her scalp pounded, the dull ache relentless.

With encouragement, Lucy swallowed a few mouthfuls of soup. Feeling like a useless toddler, she gagged and clamped her lips tightly together as the food threatened to return.

'Enough,' she said.

'That's fine. You're doing well. Would you like me to brush your hair for you before your dad arrives?'

Their eyes met as Lucy lifted a heavy hand to touch the soft locks on her shoulder.

Without a word, the nurse withdrew a brush from the drawer next to the bed and began stroking it gently through Lucy's hair, avoiding the area above her right ear. Then she dipped a cloth into the bowl of water beside them and sponged Lucy's face and hands.

'There you go. Ready and waiting for visitors,' she said cheerfully.

Lucy tried to return her smile, grateful that the nurse left the room without waiting for one. But she grimaced at the effort. Even smiling was difficult.

She took a series of deep breaths, her mind processing the events of the previous few hours. Her father and boyfriend? Who were they? A surge of panic coursed through her again. Her inability to remember anything sent heat through her while her heart pounded in her chest. Everyone was calling her Lucinda or Lucy. She had no reason to disbelieve them. The name on the tag above her bed read "Lucinda Pellegreen". But ... just who was she?

When two men entered the room an hour later, Lucy stared at them blankly, shuffling down in the bed and pulling the sheet up to her chin.

One was an older man—her father? As she stared, a familiarity about him hovered briefly. The way he sprang to her bedside and leaned over to kiss her forehead seemed reassuring, comforting even. But it took several minutes before snippets of a much younger version of her so-called-father flashed into her depleted memory bank. She relaxed—slightly.

'Robert was keen to see for himself how you are,'

her father said. 'He saw the accident happen and called the ambulance.'

Lucy studied the young man. He, too, seemed familiar, but if her father hadn't mentioned his name, she wouldn't have known who he was. There was something about the blue of his eyes though—something that warmed her. Was he her boyfriend? That's what the hospital staff had assumed but surely if he was, wouldn't he have also given her a kiss—or touched her in some way? Perhaps he was afraid of hurting her.

'W-what happened?' she stuttered. 'I can't remember.'

'We pulled down the fence in the front paddock. I'd gone to check the stock water and you were finishing up—burning the old posts. You must have decided to bring the new posts over, even though we'd planned to do it the next day.' Brent shrugged with no hint of reprimand. 'Anyway, something went wrong and you copped a whack on the head by the hook. Lucky Robert popped in on his way past and saw you fall. He called me on the two-way.'

Lucy looked at Robert. 'Thank you.'

'You're welcome, Cindy. I thought I'd check to see what gear you wanted me to bring over. I'm glad I was there.'

Her mind clouded. 'Cindy?'

A worried frown grew on her father's face as he met

her confused gaze. 'Robert's always called you Cindy. Your mother mostly called you Lucinda and he shortened it to Cindy. But, to me, you've always been Lucy.'

How confusing.

'I couldn't pronounce my "Ls" for a while. Apparently, Cindy was easier,' Robert announced apologetically.

'Oh.' Lucy didn't know what to say—or think. As her father talked, vague memories returned of an old house and a man running around a wide lawn with two giggling girls in the wheelbarrow. Was that her family? And did she have a sister?

As though reading her mind, Brent spoke again. 'Mandy said she'll call in tomorrow to see you. She's been busy with end-of-year reports and parent-teacher interviews, otherwise she would have visited sooner.'

'That's okay.'

Both men smiled then and a bolt of recognition for her father shot through her. Only he seemed much older now. The memory of a younger father remained as the sudden realisation of a missing person joined in. Her mother?

'Where's Mum?'

Her father shuffled forward in the chair and took her hand in his. 'She died, love. Not very long ago. Cancer.'

Their eyes met, his filling with tears as he spoke.

She felt nothing. No emotion and no memory.

'I'm going home tomorrow,' he continued. 'It's the weekend and Mandy will come to see you while I check on things at the farm. But I'll be back on Monday and will bring photos with me. Perhaps that will help,' he finished with a hopeful rise in his voice.

She nodded and looked up at Robert, who was still leaning against the windowsill. 'Are you going home too?'

'Yes. I've been looking after your place while your dad's been here. Drove down yesterday and I'll head home tonight.'

'Where's home?'

The exchange of disbelieving looks between the two men alarmed her. Her heart thumped wildly as terror crept in. Her inability to remember was obviously far more concerning than anyone had admitted.

Once again, her father spoke softly and slowly. 'Our farm is about four and a half hours drive away. Robert and his family are our next-door neighbours. But while you're sick, I'm staying in a motel.'

'And I slept at my aunt's place last night,' Robert added.

'Do I live on the farm?' she asked.

'At the moment, yes. You've been away for a few years though, studying nursing in Brisbane then you got a placement at the Mater hospital. You always came home when you managed a few days off though

—until you decided to have a trip to Europe and the UK.'

Her blank expression met Brent's frown.

'Don't you remember? You were living in Scotland when your mum got sick. You came home then to be with her—and me.' He choked up again.

Frustration burned through her. Why couldn't she remember any of this? Surely a trip around Europe was something she would never forget.

The three of them sat in silence for a long minute.

Drained of energy from scouring her recalcitrant memory, Lucy closed her eyes briefly. A chair scraped and her lids flew open again.

'You're tired, love. We'll go now and let you rest.' Her father bent over and kissed her forehead. 'See you again on Monday.'

As they trooped out of the room, she was gripped with a confusing sorrow that made the pain in her head thump harder.

 *ueensland, November 1990 – Mandy*

MANDY MARCHED through the hospital doors, a bunch of colourful flowers in one hand and a bag of toiletries and food treats in the other.

She glanced at her watch. *Two hours. That's all I can spare.*

The thought of the application papers sitting on her desk in her tiny, pristine Brisbane townhouse filled her mind. *I have to get that job.*

While perfectly content with the high school where she currently taught, rising to be Head of Department had become her goal—for now.

A few years in the role and I should have sufficient

experience to apply for Deputy Principal. A tiny smile crept onto her lips. Having goals and meeting them was imperative, and from an early age, Mandy had always wanted to be a teacher—and nothing had got in her way.

She pressed the lift button, stepping firmly inside as the doors opened. Wrinkling her nose, she grimaced. Why was it that hospitals always had a certain smell about them? With the amount of flowers and cleaning that went on, surely they would smell fresh. But no. There was always a lingering hint of disinfectant and often worse.

As she entered the corridor, she drew a deep breath and strode toward the room that currently contained her sister, grateful for her father's detailed directions.

Breezing into the two-bed ward, she shot a brief glance toward drawn curtains around one of the beds before approaching the other.

Lucy's hair was spread out on the pillow, her face pale. The swelling around her right eye and into her hairline was a colour palate of purple and blue hues.

'Oh my goodness. You look awful.'

Lucy's mouth twitched. 'Thanks.'

'Sorry. I didn't mean it like that,' Mandy added, giving her sister a gentle hug. She stood back and studied her more carefully. 'I suppose given the circumstances, you could be a lot worse. At least they haven't shaved your head—or not all of it, anyway.'

A chuckle burst from Lucy. 'I gather you're my sister?'

Mandy's eyes widened. 'Good grief. Dad said your memory wasn't too good but surely you remember your own sister—don't you?'

Lucy's face crumpled and she clamped her lips in a thin line as she shook her head slowly. 'I'm sort of remembering Dad a bit. But not much else. The doctor said it sometimes takes a while.'

Mandy stepped forward and wrapped gentle arms around Lucy again. 'I'm so sorry, Lucy.' A dull ache gripped deep inside her. They had never been close. Too different. But regardless of their less-than-perfect relationship while growing up, Lucy's current frailty and helplessness brought a wave of empathy to Mandy's chest. They had both recently lost their mother. They were sisters with shared blood ties. And now this. Lucy needed her.

'How are you feeling?' Mandy asked softly. 'What can I do to help you?'

'Thanks,' Lucy said. 'My headache doesn't seem to want to go away, but I suppose that's normal. The painkillers help but make me feel dopey.' She paused as their eyes met. 'I'd love you to help me wash my hair though.'

'Of course.' Mandy glanced down at the flowers on the end of the bed. 'I'll pop these in a vase first, then we'll find some nice-smelling soap and shampoo and I'll give you a hand.'

Having not showered or bathed together since they were young children—and having not lived in the same house for years—both were careful to follow privacy protocols, even if it meant the process was a little more awkward than expected. Eventually, Lucy emerged from the bathroom wearing a T-shirt and long, baggy pyjama pants, with the towel draped loosely around her head.

While Lucy sat on the side of the bed, Mandy shot along the corridor to the nurses' station to collect a hair dryer. Returning, she carefully combed out her sister's glossy brown waves.

Minutes later, with Lucy's now dry hair sitting in a fragrant waterfall on her shoulders, Mandy extracted an expensive hand and body lotion from the bag of goodies and proceeded to massage the cream into Lucy's skin.

Ignoring her sister's astonished stare, Mandy continued to pamper Lucy, pausing only when the tea trolley arrived. As Lucy's neighbour was apparently fast asleep, she joined her sister in a cup of tea and a lemon poppyseed muffin.

'Would you like me to come back again tomorrow?' Mandy said as she began packing up the pile of toiletries and stashing them in Lucy's bedside cabinet.

'Only if you want to. Dad said you live in Brisbane

and have a four-hour round trip. I'm sure you have lots to do, so I don't expect you to run up and down the range for me.'

Their gazes met for a long minute.

'Okay. Tell you what. It looks like you'll be here for another few days and I've got a couple of urgent things I've got to get done at home. How about I drive out to the farm next week and give the house a good clean? Sort your room out a bit and prepare a few meals for you and Dad?'

A glimpse of confusion crossed Lucy's face before she smiled. 'That sounds wonderful. Thank you.'

Mandy's gut clenched. *Poor Lucy. You've got no hope of going back to work if you can't remember anything, never mind returning to Scotland.* She clasped her hand in hers and squeezed it.

'Don't worry, Luce. I'm here and I'll make sure we get through this—together.'

Then she kissed her on the cheek and gave a final wave as she strode purposefully out of the room.

———

21

True to her word, Mandy arrived at "Binnalong" before lunch the following Saturday. Her application for Head of Department had been completed and submitted and now she waited—for how long she didn't know, but she hoped it wouldn't be as long as other drawn-out processes she'd experienced.

She stepped out of her smart little Mazda and reached for her overnight bag from the back seat.

Dogs barked, so she scurried inside before they could appear and jump up on her new dress.

They didn't. In fact, no one appeared so she let herself in through the unlocked veranda door and made for the room she had claimed as hers before leaving for boarding school and then university. On the rare occasions she had returned during holiday periods and for Christmas, she had tossed and turned on the firm, single bed, wishing she was back in the city. But now, the hint of her mother's perfume reached her, and she stood for several seconds in the doorway of her parents' bedroom, nostalgia biting deep.

A door crashed open, and her father's voice boomed through the house. 'That you, Mandy?'

She dropped her bag and hastened toward him, exchanging a careful hug while avoiding the grease and dust from his shirt in case it rubbed off on her clothing.

'It's good to have you here,' he said, his smile encouraging.

'No problem.' She glanced around. While the house appeared tidy, even from the centre of the living room, dust and cobwebs were evident on the sills and in the corners. Turning to face the kitchen, she frowned, taking note of the greasy sink and vaguely clean plates standing in the drainer.

'I'll change and get stuck into cleaning the house.' She glanced at her watch before peering through the dust-speckled window.

Her father stepped forward, his mouth open as if to say something, then he closed it again and headed for the kitchen sink. 'Righto. We'll have a quick cuppa then I've gotta shift a mob of cattle now the day's cooling.'

They chuckled as the iron roof crackled under the

relentless sun. As they sipped their drinks, they exchanged concerns about Lucy, discussed Mandy's plans for Christmas—evidently a five-day stay at Noosa with three of her teaching friends, none of whom had spouses or children to consider—and, at Mandy's insistence, drew up a list of jobs that needed completion in the brief twenty-four hour period she was on Binnalong.

Mandy studied her father across the table. The creases around his eyes had deepened and more had been added. A furrow was now etched down each side of his nose and mouth, suggesting stress and ... Mandy wondered, overwork?

'Are you okay, Dad?' she asked gently.

He huffed and pushed his chair back before picking up his empty mug. 'I'm fine, love. The past few weeks have been a bit more than any of us bargained for ... but that's the way it is, so I'd best be getting on with it.'

Mandy's nod of acknowledgement went unnoticed as sympathy surged through her. She glanced at her watch again as he headed for the door.

'I'll be back before dark.'

'Okay,' she said. Then, as he disappeared, she clamped her lips together and hurried toward the bedroom to change.

TWO HOURS LATER, she stood back to admire her work, grunting with exasperation as a spider crawling up the lounge curtain caught her eye.

After picking up her duster, she wacked it hard then swooped up the tiny black body with her tissue and threw it outside. Insects of all sizes, shapes, and colours were a constant annoyance to her—one of the reasons she employed a weekly house cleaner and preferred city living. However, the polished timber floor shone—its surface vacuumed and mopped, removing all traces of dust.

Two loads of sheets and towels were waiting to be hung out so, knowing they would take barely an hour to dry, she piled them into one basket, hitched it onto her hip, and tramped outside to the clothesline.

'Right. Next job,' she said aloud, fighting the tears that suddenly filled her eyes. Her words were those her mother had used a thousand times as the two of them worked together in the house each weekend. Although it was physical, Mandy hadn't minded. She enjoyed their mutual love of order and cleanliness. Lucy and her father weren't dirty or untidy but, she reasoned, their standards just weren't quite the same as hers or Leigh's.

A family of magpies settled on the veranda steps, lifted their heads, and began warbling. She smiled then, the pain inside her fading. They were her mother's favourite bird and now they were hers.

With renewed vigour, she ignored the weariness beginning to bite and, within half an hour, had a large tray of lasagne and one of chicken carbonara sitting on the stove top waiting for the oven to reach the required temperature. Then, after sliding them into the oven, Mandy stood back with her hands on her hips, breathing in the cooling breeze that wafted through the flyscreen door.

The sound of a vehicle drew close, the excited yip of dogs confirming Brent would be inside soon.

Just Lucy's bedroom to prepare now—and that can wait until tomorrow.

THE EVENING WAS GENTLE—COMPANIONABLE. As they sipped on a bottle of cabernet merlot she'd brought with her, the decades-old swing seat rocked slowly back and forth on the veranda, stirring memories of happy childhood years when her parents had whiled away the scorching summer evenings, the girls between them, as they took turns reading aloud to them. As it had been for Leigh, "Anne of Green Gables" had been one of their favourites, and every summer, the increasingly tatty book would be hauled from the bookshelf and re-read. "The Silver Brumby" was Lucy's favourite, but Mandy hadn't cared for it as much—galloping around in the Snowy Mountains was not to her taste.

'What are we going to do about Lucy?' Mandy asked firmly and the seat came to a halt.

Brent turned to her, a deep crease between his eyes. 'What do you mean?'

'What exactly are we going to do? She's not fit to go back to nursing until her memory returns—and I can't stay here to look after her. How are you going to cope?'

He shook his head slowly. 'We'll take one day at a time, love.' Leaning his head back to face the inky sky, he appeared to study the stars for a long minute before he spoke again. 'I'm sure your mother is watching over us all—she will take care of things.'

Mandy released a long, slow breath. *Here we go again. What is it about this family—will no one face up to the truth and at least try to help themselves?* 'The doctor said she has retrograde amnesia. I've looked it up and it seems that it's possible her memory won't return for weeks, or months—or even years, and when it does, she may only remember bits and pieces.'

'This is Lucy's home—just as it's yours, if you choose. She can stay and help me until she's well, then we'll see what happens next.'

Mandy straightened her shoulders and swallowed the last mouthful of wine. 'Fair enough. But just so you know, I can't be dashing out here every time things go wrong. I've got a career and my own life in Brisbane.' A brief stab of guilt softened her voice, and she trailed off. She didn't mean to sound selfish, but the farm had always come first for her parents and she was quite sure they had never understood just how much she disliked rural living. Determined this trip home would be her last for a long time—or at least until the fierce heat subsided, she stood then bent and kissed her father on the cheek. 'I'm going to bed. In the morning, I'll prepare Lucy's room for her and finish cleaning the areas I didn't get to today. Then I'm leaving—and caring for this place will be over to you and Lucy.'

Brent stared at her, his grey eyes filled with understanding and acceptance.

'I know. Go and live your life without regrets. We're all different and ... 'I'm sorry our standards ... um, are not quite the same.'

As Mandy walked away, her lip quivered. Was she being unreasonable? She didn't believe so. Her colleagues praised her for her organisational skills and efficiency. She'd never been afraid of hard work—just not the sort that involved smelly animals, dust and ... what she considered unnecessary danger.

22

After a surprisingly good night's sleep, Mandy rose as the birds began their melodious morning chorus on sunrise. The house was still, gentle snores wafting from her parents' room. She trod quietly to the veranda and stood, staring across the biscuit-dry paddocks. *Australia is such a harsh country.* She shrugged. *I suppose that's why it breeds tough men and women.*

At home in the city, she enjoyed her morning walks alongside the river. 'No reason I wouldn't here I suppose,' she muttered. She glanced down at her clean, summer sandals. 'Not in these though.'

Spotting Lucy's old sneakers, she pushed her feet into them, grateful that despite their differing shapes —Lucy was taller and thinner—at least they wore the same sized shoes.

Ignoring the whine of the dogs in their kennels, as though pleading to join her, she closed the house gate quietly and strode down the long, dusty driveway. As children, she and Lucy had often run the kilometre to and from the mailbox every morning to catch the school bus unless they could convince their father to take them on the quad bike. The distance was perfect for her walk. Especially as she still had the bathrooms and Lucy's room to clean before she drove all the way back to Brisbane. She would call in to the hospital to drop off some fresh clothes for Lucy but wouldn't stay long. She had school the following day and anyway, she would have more than done "her bit".

At the mailbox, she lifted the lid, presuming her father would have collected the mail on Friday and expecting it to be empty. But it wasn't.

After scooping up the bundle of letters, magazines, and newspapers, she tucked them under her arm and returned to the homestead.

Brent was up and had the kettle boiling when she entered. He glanced at the pile of mail and grimaced. 'I've lost track of the days. Forgot about the mail.'

Mandy handed her father the newspapers before sorting the letters. 'I'll put these bills on your office desk,' she said.

As she strolled down the hallway, she shuffled through the pile, the pale blue of an aerogramme catching her eye. She pulled it out and read Lucy's name and address on the front then, flipping it over, her eyebrows raised as she read the sender's address.

F. MacRae

Ardvasar Post Office

Ardvasar, Isle of Skye

Scotland

She placed the business mail on her father's desk and continued to Lucy's room. On her dressing table was a lidded box covered in an assortment of colourful gift wrap, most of it featuring horses and dogs. Mandy recognised it as being the one Lucy had used as a teenager to store her treasures in, so she lifted the lid and nodded at its contents. There was a fine gold chain Lucy had worn years earlier, several pens, and more letters—a whole bunch of them. Most were blue aerogrammes but there were also two Christmas cards still in their envelopes. Again, she checked the senders' addresses, nodding at the names. The aerogrammes were all from the same person—F. MacRae—and the cards were from Helen Gooding and Roslyn Bryant. They had been Lucy's best friends at boarding school. She huffed. Just like Lucy to have kept in touch with old friends. Unlike herself, who'd only had one school friend and she had moved to Perth, leaving their contact to slowly erode away. There had been a few others from school and university, but she had lost touch with them all long ago.

Following breakfast, Brent disappeared outside again, and Mandy scrubbed the bathroom and her parents' ensuite then returned to Lucy's room.

She changed the sheets before vacuuming and dusting. Then, hesitating for a moment over the letter she had dropped on the dressing table, she lifted the lid on the box and added it to the pile.

Deciding there was too much clutter on the desk for someone with memory loss to have to deal with, she tidied the wardrobe next, hanging up jeans and shirts that had slipped off their hangers and dropped to the floor and arranging them in colour-coded order. The shelf above the clothes rail was a mess of old bags, boxed shoes she doubted Lucy had worn since her school formal, and hats. She tidied them too, stacking the hats neatly on top of one another. With space to spare, she removed the scruffy box from the desk and slid it onto the shelf, pushing it into the corner and placing a shoebox on top of it.

She won't be needing that for a while, and it makes the room look untidy.

Smiling at the empty desk and clean dressing table, she gave them a final polish and ensured every drawer and cupboard door was closed firmly before plumping the pillows.

HER VISIT to the hospital had been brief. Lucy seemed pleased to see her but didn't have much to say and Mandy hadn't had time to sit and prompt her into conversation. So they had hugged each other like strangers and Mandy had continued toward Brisbane.

She was driving down the range, taking the corners carefully while listening to her favourite band, "Eagles", on the cassette player, when the aerogramme she had collected from the mailbox flashed across her mind. She had assumed F. MacRae was a girlfriend Lucy had met while travelling. *But what if the person was, or is Lucy's boyfriend?* She hadn't considered that.

A bitter taste moistened her mouth and she swallowed. If Lucy had a boyfriend, she certainly hadn't mentioned him to her—and as her younger sister, she should have, shouldn't she? Perhaps she should have left the letter on the desk. It might have helped Lucy remember something—or someone.

Mandy shuddered. No. It would NOT be a boyfriend. She had not done the wrong thing. Men were more trouble than they were worth and neither she nor her sister needed them in their lives—at least not unless they met someone exceptional and there was plenty of time for that. After all, both of them were still in their twenties.

Bile rose in her throat as the memories returned.

University. Ross. And the night she had made the

biggest mistake of her life. She had agreed to attend the party with him. She'd never been a party person, but she had so wanted to be less conspicuous. One of the crowd—and finally someone who could introduce her boyfriend to friends who didn't have one.

But over the course of the evening, the music had got louder, the alcohol more plentiful, and the smell of something everyone seemed to be smoking more intoxicating. Against her better judgement, she had let herself be swept into the crowd and with little memory of how things transpired, had found herself in a back room lying on a mattress with Ross and another guy.

Mandy couldn't call it rape. She hadn't said a word. But it had been a terrifying, painful, and messy experience—and she had been helpless to fight them.

Grabbing her clothes, she had shut herself in the bathroom, dressed hastily, and then run all the way back to the hostel in the dark, too terrified to pause.

It had been the last time she had been out with a man that wasn't her father—and the last time she had trusted another living soul.

She shook her head as a driver tooted his horn and sped past. Glancing down at the speedometer, she grimaced. *Hmm.* Sixty kilometres per hour on a national highway was a little slow—and dangerous. She pressed the accelerator and squared her shoulders.

If the aerogrammes had been sent by a man—and one Lucy had not told her about—Mandy convinced herself she had done the right thing.

Dismissing her actions as being both protective and honourable, she reassured herself the last thing either Lucy or she needed in their lives, was a man.

23

Isle of Skye, July 2024 – Fergus

FERGUS DIDN'T MIND SHEARING. It was one of those jobs that had to be done to preserve good health in his sheep. But each year, the process took him a little longer, tested unused muscles a little more, and ensured a hot bath in the evening was essential.

Callum's assistance was always welcome, and today Fergus was looking forward to his arrival more than usual. While yarding the sheep the previous evening, Callum had let slip that he'd received a lengthy call from Ingrid. Apparently the communication between him and the Australian girl had increased, bringing hope to Fergus's wounded heart.

A warm rush of blood coloured Fergus's weathered face as his chest pounded. Would this be the day he would receive news of Lucy? After thirty-four years, he had almost given up hope—but not quite. Deep within his soul, he believed one day they would meet again. Lifting his face to the grey sky, he murmured a prayer —exactly as he did every day and had done since posting his final aerogramme to Australia. Then he finished with his mantra: 'If equal affection cannot be, let the more loving be me.'

By the time Callum's Land Rover tore down the lane toward him, Fergus struggled to prevent his hands from shaking.

'Morning, Fergus. Sorry I'm a wee bit late. Been chatting to Ingrid.'

Fergus beamed. 'Again?'

'Aye.' He shot Fergus a cheeky grin. 'Had to catch her before she left for work.'

'And ... what did she have to say?'

'She's still searching. Been out to Roma for a couple of days. A bit of a hiccup, but some bloke in the post office is looking into it for us.'

'What do you mean by hiccup?'

'Apparently no one seems to know a Lucy Pellegreen and there is no property on the mail route called Binnalong.' He frowned as he shared the information. 'Something's not quite right and both Ingrid and I are determined to deepen the investigation.'

Fergus stared at him, allowing his face to soften into a wobbly smile while disappointment churned in his gut.

His shoulders sagged as he turned to the sheep. 'Right then, lad. Let's be getting the wool off these yowes.'

Fuelled by a sense of failure, Fergus dragged the first sheep from the pen, picked up the handpiece, and rhythmically removed the fleece, beginning with the ewe's belly and finishing with the final long blow from tail to shoulder. With the wool peeled off into a pile, he pulled the rope to silence the machine and stood, the ewe between his knees. Then with a flick of his hand, he pushed the animal into the empty pen and stretched. Next to him, Callum was halfway through his first sheep. Pleased to see he had a head start on his nephew, Fergus opened the gate and reached to grab his second as a vision flashed through his mind. He froze, his hand on the timber.

It was him and Lucy. In exactly the same place all those years ago, both laughing as they fought to race the other in their sheep-shearing challenge. Lucy had beaten him by a whisker—but only because his second sheep had kicked when he least expected it and he'd almost dropped the handpiece. Those brief seconds it took to regain his hold had lost him the competition.

The pain of loss surged again, a pain so great he considered bolting for the house, leaving Callum to continue, while he gathered his wits again. But then the years rolled back, and he drew a deep breath, caught the next sheep, and flipped her onto her rear-end.

Running from heartache had never worked before and now a seed of hope had been planted. He would not give up this time. Somewhere, someone must know about Lucy and her whereabouts. He would just have to be patient and hope that Ingrid uncovered something soon.

24

 ueensland, July 2024 – Ingrid

THE CALL CAME when Ingrid least expected it.

Her father had rallied over the previous few days, managing to swallow a few mouthfuls of thickened fluids, even though recognition of both his wife and children had vanished altogether.

But none of them had expected him to pass away in his sleep—the result of a heart attack.

Ingrid was once again on the days-off portion of her roster—a blessing she was thankful for as she and Vonnie cried buckets of tears, doubling in quantity when Rod and Laura joined them.

Eventually resigning themselves to the circumstances, they moved on to arranging the final goodbyes and attempted to return to some semblance of normal. It was days later before she managed another lengthy phone call with Callum. Although exchanging increasing numbers of messages, she relished their video call, his smile twisting her heart with joy when he connected. After the usual greetings, she shared her festering doubts about the information given by Dalgonally's new governess.

'I thought I'd go out there again,' she said. 'Only this time I'll ring the station first and arrange a meeting with the owner—if that's possible.'

'Good idea. Poor Fergus was shattered by the time we finished shearing. He hardly spoke on the final day, so I pestered him a bit, trying to jolly him—as much as Fergus can ever be jollied.'

They both laughed.

'I thought he'd send me packing, but he didn't.' Callum's voice softened.

Ingrid leaned closer to her phone screen. 'And?' she asked, sensing something important was about to be revealed.

'He told me about a challenge he and Lucy had shared all those years ago. Apparently she could shear a sheep as well as any man. He took up the challenge —and lost!' He laughed again and an intense rush of emotion jammed in her throat as her admiration for this woman grew.

'That's exactly the reason I will not give up. Lucy must have been—and hopefully still is—a strong, capable woman. So where could she be? And why can't I find her?' she said.

'Have you checked the register of marriages?' Callum said hopefully.

'Oh my goodness. No! I haven't thought about that.'

'It's worth a try.'

They chatted for a further half hour before ending the call with a promise to talk again after Ingrid had made enquiries with the Registry of Births, Deaths and Marriages.

Despite the loss of her father and coping with her mother's emotions as well as her own as she adjusted, hope blossomed again, and Ingrid felt like skipping around the room like a young child—cautiously, of course.

ONE LOOK at the following two week's roster had Ingrid's hopes sinking to her boots. The chance of revisiting Roma wouldn't be happening any time soon. 'Barely enough time off to plan another trip, let alone enjoy it,' she grumbled to her mother the following evening. 'The only break of two consecutive days off is straight after my night shifts—and somewhere in that period I'll need to sleep.'

Huffing with frustration, she regaled the disappointing phone conversation she'd had during her lunchbreak with the Registry of Births, Deaths and Marriages.

'They won't even allow me to apply for information because marriage records contain personal information about two people—apparently.' She grunted as the hint of a grin hovered on her mouth. 'Of course it does.'

'What about enquiring if there is a death certificate?' Vonnie suggested gently. 'Not that I expect that would be easy either. Look at all the paperwork we're having to do since your dad died, and we're his family.'

'Yeah. I thought about that too. But we don't know what her married name is.'

'Of course you don't. But there's no harm in making enquiries—in whichever format is required. Start by finding out if there is a registered death for this Lucy Pellegreen.'

Ingrid looked at her mother as if an illuminated halo had just encircled her.

'You're a genius.' She gave Vonnie a quick hug. 'I'll check it before I ring Callum again.'

As she trawled through the online information, hope once again swelled as she read the fine detail. It seemed anyone could apply for a death certificate. They just had to complete the application and submit it, together with a fee. How long the result would take to be returned remained to be seen. But ... anything was worth a try.

ueensland, November 1990 – Lucy

BEFORE CLIMBING out of the passenger seat, Lucy waited, casting a long look around the yard.

Dogs barked, their high-pitched excitement evident.

She smiled. Dogs were her favourite animal. And horses. She liked sheep too, but she couldn't see any. Perhaps they were in paddocks out of sight of the house.

Home. She slid out of the car and turned to face it. Memories flooded back and she almost collapsed with relief. She hadn't lost it after all!

Her father had disappeared momentarily,

returning with dogs leaping around his feet—one black and white and the other a faded black and tan with a grey muzzle. As soon as they saw her, they rushed toward her, yipping with joy.

'Indie! Duke!' Her father beamed at her as he called them. 'Do you remember these two?'

'I think so.' She exhaled a long breath and looked into her father's eyes. 'I just couldn't remember their names.'

His gaze softened as their eyes met, and she nodded. 'Yes, I remember Mum. I look a lot like her, don't I? Same brown hair and eyes.' Then she frowned. 'I remember nursing too—and saving for my overseas trip. But ... I can't remember what happened after that?'

'The doctor said that's not unusual. He told you not to worry. Sometimes it takes a while—years even for everything to return. It seems brains are like that. We have to be patient and every now and then something will come back to you.'

She smiled. 'The photos were a good idea. Thanks for that.'

He nodded.

Flicking through the albums together had triggered the return of small snippets of her past. Her sister had visited and, although she had been kind and had helped her shower and brought her beautiful flowers, she had felt more like an acquaintance from childhood rather than her only sister. But when her father had arrived and they had poured through the pages, her childhood had returned—mostly anyway. There were people she didn't recognize, and some occasions that were fuzzy in her mind, but gradually over the two weeks since the accident, recollections of school, the farm, and the occasional family holiday had become clearer, helped by the pictures.

'Come on then. Let's unpack and have a nice cup of tea,' Brent said, leading the way up the steps onto the veranda.

The familiar smell hit her first. A hint of camphor and lavender as she walked past the linen cupboard. Then a musty scent as she passed the book-filled nook her father used as a study. She continued down the hallway, automatically turning into a compact bedroom containing a single bed covered in a brightly-coloured doona, an old wooden dressing table bearing an antique, lidded trinket bowl, and a photo of the four of them—her parents, sister, and herself. In the corner beside the wardrobe was a small desk, it's surface clean and smelling of furniture polish. Tucked underneath it was a fragile-looking office chair.

After dropping her bag on the bed, she glanced at her reflection in the mirror. Fingering the right side of her face gently, her eyes widened at the multi-coloured skin covering almost half of her face. Spinning away from the sight, she wandered to the window and stared through the sparkling clean glass. Surrounded by parched, brown paddocks, a small, weed-filled vegetable garden, a straggling rose bed, and a bright green lawn appeared to provide the only hint of moisture. *Drought?*

Her eyes narrowed as vague images of empty dams and regular trips in the farm ute to turn on massive irrigation taps hovered.

'Cup of tea's ready!' her father called down the hallway.

Turning away from the window, she resisted taking another look in the mirror. The ugly bruising reminded her of something to do with horses from years earlier. The result of a fall perhaps? She shrugged. It didn't matter. Bruised skin eventually returned to normal. It was what happened beneath the bruise that mattered most.

She wandered back to the kitchen.

'Everything alright, love?' Brent said.

She drew a deep breath and sat down. 'Yeah. I guess so.' Screwing up her nose, she exhaled noisily. 'I just wish I could remember ... everything.'

'The doctor said retrograde amnesia can take a while to recover from. The best thing is to relax and enjoy life and it will return—eventually.' He shot her a worried look. 'If you feel up to it, tomorrow we'll go for a drive around the farm. Perhaps that will jog a few memories.'

'What about my job, Dad? Are they expecting me back at work?'

He shook his head sadly. 'No, love. You resigned almost a year ago. You wanted to travel—and you did.'

They sat in silence, sipping their tea for long minutes before Brent spoke again. 'Perhaps one of those travel shows might be on television later. You used to love watching them. Gave you ideas of where you wanted to go.'

'Did I?' She sank her head into her hands.

'Don't worry about it now, love. You're tired. Perhaps you should rest while I check the troughs. And the rub. Now the hot weather is here, so are the flies.'

Their gaze met, hers a blank stare. 'What about the sheep?'

Shaking his head, he huffed patiently. 'No sheep now. We switched to cattle when you were living in Brisbane, so I suppose you missed a lot of it. We couldn't justify keeping them any longer as prices were plummeting.'

Vague memories wandered back and, although the news was gloomy, a leap of hope fizzed through her as the recollections returned. 'That's right. A lot of people had to shoot their stock, but you had already sold yours before things got that bad.'

A beaming smile widened on his face. 'Yes!'

She returned his optimistic smile and pushed her

chair back. 'I've got a headache, so I'll lie down for a while and see if any other memories return.'

'Righto. I'll be back as soon as possible. I've got one of those lasagnes Mandy made out of the freezer for dinner. It just needs heating, so leave it to me.'

She nodded, waiting and watching as he pulled on his boots, picked up his hat, and strode toward the old Toyota ute sitting near the gate. Then she turned and trod back to her room, her feet silent on the polished boards.

The horses in the front paddock caught her eye and she sighed. Perhaps everything would come back to her soon and life could progress. Now she was home, snippets were returning. School days. Riding horses with Robert. Nursing—and even the sheep being sold. One day she would remember more. *Dad is right. I just have to be patient.*

The heat of the day was easing now, the afternoon sun sliding slowly westward. 'I'll give the horses some attention,' she said aloud. 'I'm sure that will help.'

And with cautious enthusiasm, she took two tablets, ignoring her plan to rest, and walked slowly outside.

WHILE STROKING THE HORSES' noses, Lucy breathed in

their smell—dust, sweat, and a hint of slobbery, well-chewed lucerne hay.

Despite the gaps in her memory, thoughts of happier times mustering with her father and racing Robert on their horses at pony club popped into her mind. She smiled and ran her hand down the neck of the bay gelding.

'You and I had some fun, didn't we—although it's a while ago now.'

The palomino nudged Lucy's shoulder as though reminding her of her presence.

'Alright, Goldie. I haven't forgotten you.' She reached out and ran a hand down the mare's neck, combing the tangled forelock out with her fingers as a spark of excitement exploded. 'I remembered your name!'

She leaned forward and rested her face against the mare. 'Tomorrow I'll groom you both,' she whispered. 'Today ... well, just let's get through today and hope tomorrow will be better.'

26

———

In the weeks leading up to Christmas, clouds threatened but not a drop of rain landed on the ground. Brent was becoming morose, his previously positive attitude now subdued. Lucy was worried about him. While she understood how grief affected people differently, she was sure it was more than her mother's death. Something was concerning him—and she needed to find out what it was.

Sprawled in front of the television that evening, Lucy glanced across at her father. The fans above them churned with the regular thump that was not exactly distracting but did require the volume to be increased if they wanted to hear every word emitted from whatever show they were watching. Although Brent's attention appeared to be focused on the TV, Lucy was sure his mind was light-years away from *The Flying Doctors*.

'Dad?'

She waited for a beat, but he made no movement.

'Dad!'

He jumped then and stared at her with wide eyes. 'Yes?'

'Something's bothering you. Do you want to talk about it?'

He heaved a sigh.

She walked over to the television and switched it off then returned to the couch and rested her hands in her lap, waiting.

'It's the farm.'

Her eyebrows shot up. 'The drought?'

He shook his head. 'That isn't helping, but no ... it's more than that.' Lifting his gaze to meet hers, he straightened as though preparing to deliver a report.

'Go on,' she urged.

'I suppose I'm missing your mum. We had so many plans. She was the ideas person, and I was always ... well, the follower I suppose. She wanted to branch out into alternative methods of farming. Put our eggs in more than one basket is what she meant, I guess.'

'I get it, Dad.' Having not been part of any discussions about the farm's future, Lucy had simply expected it to always be there. Her home to retreat to when she needed it. But now she could see there was far more to it than coping with the weather and doing their best to make a living from the cattle and crops. There was a lifestyle to balance—and the loss of Leigh and her own accident had put more obstacles in Brent's way than he was currently able to cope with.

'You want to stay here though, don't you?' A frisson of fear wormed its way inside her. While she had managed living in Brisbane for the duration of her training, the farm had always been her bolt hole—her home and her solace. Life without it wouldn't be worth living.

'I do. Of course. But without Leigh, now I'm not so sure.'

A lump in Lucy's throat formed and she tried to swallow it as she stared at him, her face soft. They had been so happy. Never wealthy but content in their own cocooned way. With the wide land, blue skies, horses, stock, and a loving family, it had been all they'd needed. But now the time had come for change—and she suddenly realised that lapses of memory or not, it was over to her to put things right. At least as much as possible.

'Okay,' she said, getting to her feet. 'I'll get paper and a pen, and we'll make a start on fixing this.'

Ignoring Brent's confused frown, she marched into the study nook, picked up a pen and pad, and returned to the lounge.

'Tell me about Mum's plans—or dreams.'

'Well, she was right into changing our farming methods. You know, reducing chemicals for a start. We've been doing that. For the last two years, we've rotated the crops, slashed the paddocks, and reduced the number of cattle in order for the native grasses to regenerate. We built those new fences so we could cell graze. And, of course, your mother has ordered and planted more trees than this place has ever seen. But now, with this drought, it doesn't matter what we do— nature is against us.'

Lucy knelt beside him and wrapped her arms around him in an awkward hug. 'Aww, Dad. I understand how much you want to follow the plan, but perhaps now we need to rethink our strategies—especially since they're predicting this El Nino could go on for months or even years.'

Over a cup of tea and with Lucy's dogged determination and scribbled notes, by ten o'clock that night, a new plan was in place. They would reduce the cattle and keep only the best breeders and bulls—thus saving more land being churned to dust than necessary and enabling them to ration feed, hopefully eliminating the need to delve into their meagre savings or worse—increasing the mortgage. They would also minimise fuel consumption by not following other farmers in the area who insisted on ploughing the land "so we're ready to plant as soon as the rain comes".

'We'll concentrate on looking after the trees, even

though I know they won't bring in any money. At least then, no matter what happens, there will be a legacy here for the next generation. Who knows what timber will be required in thirty or forty years.' She paused and drew a deep breath. 'Also, I'm going to apply for a job at the hospital.'

'But,' Brent spluttered. 'You're not well yet. You've barely driven since your accident and working in town will mean you'll be in the car for almost two hours every day.'

'I'm fine, Dad. If I lived in the city, it could take every bit of that to get to work. Anyway, I may have forgotten a few bits and pieces of my life but it's slowly returning and perhaps getting back into nursing will help me—that is if they'll let me?'

Her boldness waned as she considered the doctor's comments. He had suggested she wouldn't be fit to return to work until her headaches eased and she regained her memory—but she knew he had been referring to returning to her previous duties as a registered nurse in a large hospital. What if she changed tack and instead applied for something in the aged care facility where she could work under supervision? They were always crying out for staff— and a willing and qualified nurse would surely be better than no one, even if she couldn't remember the previous few months' activities. At least she would be able to bring in enough income to tide them over the drought—no matter how long it continued for.

'WE'D LOVE you to join us for Christmas,' the voice boomed down the phone the following morning as Lucy was about to walk out the door.

She blinked at Finlay's commanding tone. Their neighbour, Robert's father, had always been domineering, his large stature and big voice a little frightening. But his community spirit was generous to a fault, and it wouldn't be the first time the Venables' home had overflowed at Christmas with what he termed "orphans" from around the district. If he or his wife, Belinda, heard of a neighbour or friend having a quiet Christmas with little or no family, they were swooped up in the Venables' encompassing arms and added to the crowded veranda that surrounded the massive Dalgonally homestead.

'Thanks, Mr Venables,' she said. 'That would be lovely.'

Before she could add more, he roared again. 'Call me Fin. You're all adults now, so we can cut the formalities. Anyway, I hear young Robert's more than a bit keen to include you in our family. This'll be a great start to new beginnings.'

'Umm ... thank you. I'll ring Belinda later to see

what we can bring.' Her chest thumped. Was Robert clutching at straws when he'd suggested his interest in her to his family? They had been friends for years but … she wracked her addled brain. Had there ever been a suggestion of more than that?

The clang of the phone jangled in her ear as Fin hung up. That was it? She and her father had been summoned to Dalgonally for Christmas lunch—and no one refused!

A WEEK LATER, she sat at the sixteen-seat table running almost the length of the Dalgonally homestead veranda. A second table formed the head of a T where Finlay, Belinda, and two of their four sons sat. At the opposite end, four children perched around a tiny table, half the height of the adults' chairs.

Daunted by the crowd, Lucy squirmed as the Venables family focused on her, bringing up events from her childhood that she had no recollection of. It seemed she and Robert had been competitive, both vying for first place at any pony club sports days. Although some of it rang true, she was sure the depth of friendship between them was exaggerated. Her gaze slid sideways to Robert as she sensed his eyes on her. There was a perception of familiarity about him, but she couldn't quite put her finger on why she felt no emotion. No fluttering in her stomach. Not even a hot flush of embarrassment. She glanced down the table to where her father was listening intently to something Jeff Longford, a middle-aged bachelor renowned for his love of alcohol and exhaustingly lengthy conversations, was saying.

Poor Dad. Her mouth twitched in an attempted smile. *You'll be deaf by the time the day's over.*

'I hear you're starting work in aged care next week, Lucy,' Belinda said, jolting Lucy's attention back to the present.

'Oh. Umm, yes.' She didn't elaborate on the upsetting interview she'd had with the hospital board. *"Until your memory has returned, we're reluctant to employ you in case you're put in an unsupervised position and make a mistake. I'm sure you understand how difficult that could be for both you, and the patient."* She'd nodded in silence, biting back tears of despair and frustration.

She'd gone straight to the café afterwards and ordered a chicken sandwich and a strong coffee. Then she'd driven to the aged care home and, within an hour, had returned to her car, her head spinning with elation and a start date of the third of January 1991.

Belinda reached over and patted Lucy's hand. 'You'll be perfect there. What with all that training you've done—and you have a sweet nature. The residents will love you.'

Lucy's eyes widened in disbelief. How would

Belinda know what she was like? She may have mixed with the Venable boys as children, but now … except for seeing more of Robert over the past few weeks than she remembered in her youth, she knew very little about the "grown up" family—and they knew even less about her. At least that's what she hoped!

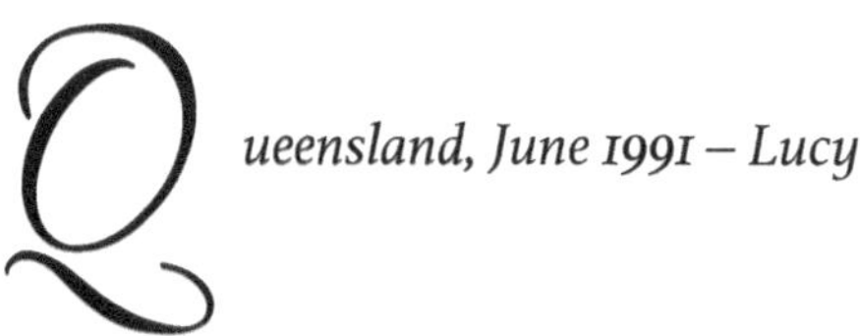

27

Queensland, June 1991 – Lucy

SHE STOOD on the veranda and gazed over the paddocks as the white ute approached the house gate. The last six months had sped by in a flash. With both the Venables family and her father's encouragement, Robert had spent increasingly long days "helping" at Binnalong—and the relationship between him and Lucy had developed. No longer the competitive children on horseback, she looked forward to seeing him each morning as he arrived either in a ute or on a quad bike. They had continued to plant trees together, drove around the farm checking stock and fences, mustered and drenched the cattle—and had even spent weeks sanding and repainting the outside of the Binnalong homestead in comfortable camaraderie under Brent's increasingly hopeful gaze.

It had been over the Easter weekend when Robert had asked her to marry him. A surprisingly good fall of rain had ensured the dams once again glistened in the early autumn sunshine, and they had taken the opportunity to have a picnic and swim before they opened the gate and let the cattle in.

Although the drought was continuing, the few summer showers had boosted everyone's moods, and although Robert's proposal came as a surprise to Lucy, she'd accepted, relieved that whatever it was that had been hanging in the back of her mind had floated away. Her memory still contained gaps, the most significant being the year leading up to her accident. But apart from recognising the occasional European tourist attraction or a pretty English country scene that seemed familiar, Lucy had dismissed them as being places she must have visited on her overseas sojourn.

Robert leapt up the steps and grabbed her in his arms, lifting her off the ground and swinging her around. She giggled, enjoying the moment of joy, despite her misgivings.

'Only one week to go.'

'I know.' She pointed to the cabin under construction on the other side of the machinery shed. 'By the time we get back from our honeymoon, that will be finished and Dad will have moved in—I hope, anyway.'

'Are you sure you want to stay here? I mean, the cottages Dad's had built at home are modern and we could make one of them exactly the way we want it.'

She shook her head, astounded that he would bring up the subject again, despite the arrangements made weeks earlier. 'Absolutely. Dad doesn't want to be left trying to look after this place. Mum and I have always loved it, and I couldn't leave him here anyway. I owe it to her. He's excited about the cabin—and this way we will all have more privacy and can still work the two properties together as our fathers have suggested.'

He held his palms up in a gesture of surrender. 'Okay. Just checking.'

'You're not exactly moving far from home. Ten minutes, fifteen at most from one house to the other across the back lane, especially now you've installed the cattle grids. No more gates to have to open and shut.' She smiled at him again as she spoke. The past few weeks had included a whirlwind of family discussions and plans. She had felt powerless in the tornado of excitement that surrounded her—even if her stomach still flipped at the thought of being married.

'Okay, so are you ready to join us at Dalgonally for our final pre-wedding dinner?'

She nodded. 'Dad said he won't be long. Just getting through the shower then he'll follow.'

He grabbed her hand. 'Great. Come on then—soon-to-be-Mrs-Venables.'

As she slid into the passenger seat, the familiar whisper of doubt filtered through her insides. She brushed it away as his deep blue eyes met hers. It was his irises that had done it. The vivid shade that hung in the back of her mind. She'd known the love of her life had those same sapphire-coloured eyes—and unless she had made a dreadful mistake, they could only belong to Robert.

As they rattled past the struggling crops, Lucy reflected on her father's positivity. Brent had assured her the Easter rain was a good omen and Leigh was watching over them. Even if the barley never got to a head, it would provide good winter feed for their remaining cattle. That and the chickpea crop he had risked planting would see them through another year if they were careful.

Over the months of sharing the weekly dinner at Dalgonally, Lucy began to feel like a part of the Venables family. Snippets of memory returned as events of the past were discussed and while watching a recent travel program on television, Lucy had been delighted to recognise familiar German landmarks. At first, she'd presumed it was because she'd seen pictures in magazines and in the windows of travel agencies. But then, one night when the program featured Bavaria, she knew she had been there. It had been toward the end of the European winter, and she could almost feel the frosty air touch her face.

Spending more time with regular male company had eased much of Brent's depression too—a problem Lucy was relieved and delighted to witness.

Both she and Brent looked forward to their regular inter-family get-togethers, and with only infrequent chats with Mandy, she looked forward to catching up with Matthew's wife, Kylie and their young son, Dylan. With the exception of the staff and patients she cared for during her three days a week at the nursing home, Kylie was the only other female she saw on a regular basis. She valued the friendship of the kind, cheerful woman only a few years older than herself.

The rest of each week sped past and sometimes she was sure there wouldn't be enough hours in the day to get done what she wanted to. Farm work, maintaining the lawn and what little garden was surviving the drought, and caring for the precious trees took most of her outside time, even with Robert's help. Although Mandy had returned to the farm infrequently since the accident, Lucy never missed giving the house a good clean each Friday—

just in case her critical sister decided to spring an unexpected visit on them and critique her cleanliness.

AS THEY APPROACHED the Dalgonally homestead, Lucy released a long, slow breath. The house was huge, it's deep, insect-screened verandas encompassing all four sides of the building, allowing ample shade from the scorching summer sun. The long side facing the irrigated lawn, shady trees and central rose garden provided oodles of space for the massive table that allowed all family, staff, and friends to dine free of flies —and a safe runway for little Dylan to scoot up and down the boards on his trike.

Fifty metres away, on the far side of the outbuildings, two neat cottages in their final stages of construction shone in the evening light. One had been designated for Matthew and Kylie as, although the homestead was spacious, their little family was growing with baby number two due soon. Kylie had begged for a place of their own and, with pressure and understanding from Belinda, Finlay had agreed to add to his kingdom and had arranged for the construction of not one but two new dwellings. The second would be used for staff quarters during the busy periods of harvesting and mustering—"Unless Robert and Lucy change their minds and move in," Finlay had remarked hopefully.

'No way,' Lucy had said when she and Robert discussed it afterwards. 'We've been through all this before. Dad needs me. Our boundaries are joined, and you'll be working on both properties so it shouldn't matter where you live—but I am staying on Binnalong.'

There had been a few moments silence after her declaration, but she didn't care. Robert was the one who, with his parents' encouragement, had pressed for their marriage to happen sooner rather than later. She'd wanted longer to think about it. But, with the frailty she occasionally felt without her memory, she eventually agreed with her father. Robert wanted to care for her. She wondered if in some way he felt a little responsible for her accident. Was it possible she would have noticed the swinging hook if she hadn't been distracted by the headlights of his ute? She wasn't sure. Or was it an admission of something being absent from their relationship? If she truly loved him, wouldn't she feel a need, a desire, or even a desperation to be together always no matter the situation? She kept the thought to herself. Perhaps she was dreaming of something that didn't exist? She was confident that Robert loved her, was a kind and gentle person much like her father, and they were good friends.

Would that be enough? She hoped so.

THEIR WEDDING DAY dawned cold but with the clear blue skies that only a frosty winter's day could bring.

With the quantity of family and friends the Venables had invited too numerous to consider a small wedding on the Binnalong lawn, Lucy had resigned herself to fitting in with whatever Finlay and Belinda arranged. She had spent three Saturday mornings with Laurel, an old friend of her mother's who also happened to be a clever seamstress, and an elegant, satin-lined chiffon gown had been pieced lovingly together—and a soft lavender version made for Mandy, her one and only bridesmaid.

A heaviness sat deep in her body as she turned slowly in front of the mirror. She wished her mother was with her—and her two best friends, Helen and Roslyn. Although only having connected once since her return home—and that was filled with condolences from them both after hearing via the grapevine of her mother's sudden death—her old friends from the years of sharing a room at boarding school had kept in touch since they finished their education in a spasmodic but intense kind of way. With heavily pregnant Helen living two-days' drive away and Roslyn on a cruise in the Pacific, neither of them had been available to attend her wedding.

'Come on, dreamboat,' Mandy said impatiently.

'Dad's waiting.' She thrust a bouquet toward Lucy and looked her up and down. 'Perfect.' Then she turned and marched toward the kitchen with her smaller bouquet in one hand and the other holding up the front of her dress, enabling her to take longer strides.

Dalgonally was adorned with fairy lights and tubs of flowers placed strategically around the lawns, camouflaging the bare branches of trees and frosted gardens. A white archway led to rows of chairs filled with guests of all ages, sizes, and standards of dress, and a narrow red carpet lay along the lawn in the centre, ending in front of a small table. To one side, a round-faced woman in an elegant but neutral-coloured dress faced Lucy as she and her father began walking into what, to Lucy, felt like an entrance into Tolkien's magical mountain in *The Lord of the Rings*.

Robert and his brother Simon beamed at them. She focused on the blue of Robert's eyes and forced a smile on her face.

I have no idea if I'm doing the right thing here, Mum. But whatever happens, I'll make it work.

Q ueensland, July 2024 – Ingrid

INGRID'S DAY began as every other did when she was on a run of day shifts. She and Vonnie dressed warmly and struck out for an hour's walk, breathing in the frosty morning air and sharing occasional items of conversation but mostly striding side by side in companionable silence.

'Only one more shift, Mum, then I've got four days off. How do you feel about coming with me on a trip to Roma?'

'Lovely—especially at this time of the year. I don't think I could cope with the heat in summer.' Vonnie chuckled.

Ingrid returned her smile. The change in her mother had been dramatic. Although they had all grieved in their own way, Ingrid realised the toll that her father's illness had taken on her mother had been heavy. Once he'd gone and they had processed the whole, sad prelude to his death, Vonnie had slept better, eaten more and, after Ingrid's initial coaxing, had grown to enjoy her new routine—especially the fresh-brewed coffee at the hill-top café toward the end of their walk.

Back in the comfortable brick home, the fire glowed warmly as Ingrid prepared for another day at the hospital.

With her lunch packed and her bag over her shoulder, she kissed her mother goodbye and closed the door behind her.

Driving through the morning traffic was slow but nothing like living in Brisbane. Amazed that Rod and Laura loved Queensland's capital city so much, her mind drifted to the Isle of Skye, and she smiled at the comparison, allowing the vision of Skye's rugged mountains and picturesque crofts to fill her mind. She jumped as the car behind her tooted with impatience, waved an apology, and accelerated away, dragging her attention from Scotland and Callum to what might be waiting for her at the hospital.

As always, the emergency department was full,

choked with people of all ages, nationalities, and degrees of complaints and illnesses.

The morning flew as Ingrid and the team of doctors and nurses dealt with the constant stream of patients, and by the time there was a slight easing in the congestion, Ingrid was famished. She checked with the nurse manager before grabbing her lunch and attempting to exit the hospital, seeking a quiet corner in the grounds to sit, eat, and read her book for half an hour.

While crossing the front entrance floor, a woman rushed toward her, clearly in a hurry and with a flustered appearance that Ingrid witnessed every hour of every day. A visitor from out of town no doubt.

'Excuse me,' the woman said. 'Can you help? I'm looking for a colleague who had an accident.'

Ingrid blinked. 'How long ago was the accident? Has the patient been admitted?'

'I don't know. She's a teacher from our school—here with a group of children on an excursion—and I believe she tripped on the coach step and may have broken her ankle.'

'I see,' Ingrid said calmly. 'Follow the signs to the emergency department and someone there will be able to ... advise you.' Her words trailed off as she stared at the name badge on the woman's smart navy blazer. *Ms Pellegreen.*

'Thank you.' The lady stepped forward, about to

charge off again when Ingrid reached out and touched her arm.

'Ms Pellegreen?'

'Yes.' She stopped and met Ingrid's stare. 'Do I know you?'

Ingrid shook her head. 'No. But perhaps you may be able to help me?'

'I can't think why—and I'm sorry, I need to locate my colleague.' She tut-tutted. 'I wouldn't normally rush to the hospital if a staff member was injured— that is the responsibility of the school nurse and, of course, Queensland Health. However, I decided I would call in to ensure she has what she needs as I had a meeting to attend here in Toowoomba this morning.'

She attempted to move again when Ingrid fell in beside her. 'I'll come with you and see what we can find out about your friend.' Hesitating for only a split second and conscious that this was the closest she'd been in her search for Lucy, she took a deep breath. At least the surname matched. 'Do you know of a woman called Lucy Pellegreen?'

Ms Pellegreen stopped so suddenly, Ingrid was two strides ahead before she halted and turned to face her.

'Yes. She's my sister.'

'Oh?'

'Only she's not Lucy Pellegreen anymore. Her husband always called her Cindy. They'd been friends since childhood, so after they married I guess everyone else followed suit, except me of course. Being married, her surname changed too—unlike many these days, she was happy to take her husband's name.'

The official-looking woman sniffed as though the thought of changing a name triggered a bad taste in her mouth. Then, narrowing her eyes, she met Ingrid's astonished gaze. 'Why do you want to know?'

'I've been looking for her ... on behalf of an old friend of hers.' Ingrid looked around, her stomach fluttering wildly. She needed to talk to this woman at length. She mustn't leave.

Taking Ms Pellegreen by the arm, she forged ahead, prepared to forgo her lunchbreak to follow this potentially extraordinary lead.

'We'll find out where your friend is, and then I'll take you to her myself if you could spare just a few minutes of your time to share Lucy's details with me?'

It took no time to establish the injured teacher had been triaged and taken for X-rays.

'I'll show you where that is, and perhaps we could chat while you wait for her?' Ingrid crossed her fingers, silently begging the woman to cooperate, despite the frown of suspicion on the other woman's face.

'I can't imagine why this friend you're helping hasn't spoken to Lucy herself—if she really is a friend.' Her voice took on an authoritarian tone and Ingrid immediately felt herself shrink as if being questioned by a police officer—or a school principal.

'The friend is not here in Australia. That's why I'm helping him, not her. By the way, my name is Ingrid. Ingrid Sloane.' They reached the lift. Ingrid pushed the button and held out her hand.

The woman took it. 'Mandy Pellegreen.'

'Can you tell me if Lucy is alive and living in Queensland?'

'Yes, to both questions. She's on the farm where we grew up. Our parents have passed on and so has her husband. So she lives there with her son—for the moment anyway.'

Ingrid frowned. 'Binnalong?'

'Yes. Only it's not called that anymore. She married into the family who own the property next door—the farm that Binnalong had once been part of and now is again.'

'Confusing.'

Mandy nodded. 'I suppose so. Apparently it seemed easier at the time for Lucy to agree with the dominating party.'

Ignoring the woman's resigned tone, Ingrid rushed on. 'I drove out there to see if I could track her down. However, I only had the name and address she used in 1990 and no one was able to help me.'

'Really? I don't see why not. Everyone knows she was Lucy Pellegreen before she married and became Cindy Venables.'

'Well. Not everyone it seems. Unfortunately the owners of the property were not home when I visited. I spoke to a girl who had recently been employed as a governess, but she couldn't help me. I asked at the post office in town too, but none of the staff were able to help.'

Mandy huffed. 'I see.'

They arrived at the correct floor and stepped out of the lift.

Ingrid strode alongside Mandy until they reached the X-ray department waiting room. 'Would you like me to wait with you?'

'No thank you. I'll be fine.' Her demeanour softened as she searched in her bag then handed Ingrid a card. 'If you have trouble contacting Lucy, send me a message. Meanwhile, I'll let her know I've bumped into you.'

Ingrid smiled and thanked her before looking down at the card. The name of a prominent Brisbane school headed the title with "Principal, Ms Mandy Pellegreen" underneath it. Not a surprise. Her guess had been accurate.

She turned to leave.

'Before you go. What was the name of Lucy's friend who's looking for her?'

'Fergus MacRae. He lives on the Isle of Skye.'

Colour drained from Mandy's face. She staggered to a vacant chair and plonked herself down.

'Are you alright?' Ingrid asked, astonished at the sudden change in Mandy.

Mandy flapped a hand at her as though determined not to share the cause of her condition. 'Of course. I'm fine.' She looked around, Ingrid following her gaze to the water cooler. 'I've had a busy morning and it's catching up with me. That's all. A drink of water is all I need.'

Ingrid hurriedly filled a disposable cup and handed it to her.

'Thank you. You can go now,' Mandy said.

In stunned silence, Ingrid took a backward step then turned and left the room.

 *ueensland, July 2024 – Lucy*

THE RUMBLE of the Prado faded into the distance, a trail of fine dust settling silently in the wake of the horse float being towed behind it.

Lucy smiled to herself, lost for a moment in the peace that followed. A lifetime ago it had been her and her father heading off to compete in a campdraft competition. Now it was her son and his fiancée.

Reflecting on the years in between, she shook her head slowly. So much change. There had been lots of happy times. But there had also been many days, weeks, and months filled with a sense of loss and emptiness.

A rhythmic drip of melting frost from the shed roof beyond the garden beat time with her heart. She enjoyed winter. Others complained about the cold. Didn't want to get out of bed early. But she was the opposite. The crisp air. The mist that hung over the paddocks. And the warmth and companionship of a wood fire each evening all combined to remind her it was her favourite time of the year. Sometimes as she stared into the flames, a strange aroma drifted through her memory. She couldn't identify it but was certain it belonged to a joyful time somewhere in her past.

A black and white border collie leaned against her leg, and she looked down at it.

'Want to go for a walk, Jet?'

The tail thumped on the wooden veranda as the dog squirmed with joy.

'Let me get my boots and jacket on then. Adam and Meg won't be back until Sunday night, so it's just you and me for the next three days.'

She wasn't sure why she'd called the writhing bundle of fur Jet when Adam had given him to her for Christmas. It seemed appropriate—and from some-where deep in her mind, she felt it had been the name of another dog she had loved, even if she couldn't remember who's dog it had been.

Minutes later, the two of them strolled through a gate leading to rows of flourishing native trees and shrubs. Fingering the new shoots of vibrant yellow wattle, she paused. The early plantations of trees her mother had started now encompassed every boundary on the property, and here in the twenty-acre paddock close to the house, Lucy had added hundreds more, planting them in neat rows, frantically working herself into an exhausted stupor. She referred to the year as her "Annus Horribilis", much like Queen Elizabeth had admitted after the year when parts of Windsor Castle were destroyed by fire, Princess Diana's personal struggles were aired to the world, and three of her four children separated from their partners.

All the things that have happened in thirty-three years.

The arrival of their only child, Adam, had filled their marriage with love and delight. It had been a difficult birth and there had been no more. She hadn't minded. Adam was enough and with his cousins only a few minutes away, he was never short of company.

Adam had been in his final year of primary school when Finlay announced that he, Robert, and Brent would be attending "beef week" in Rockhampton. They had enjoyed the event on several occasions but this time they wouldn't be driving. Instead, they would fly in the brand-new Cessna, reducing the travel time by hours. Finlay had wanted Matthew to join them—the perfect men's week away—but Matthew had refused. Kylie had been heavily pregnant with twins, and he didn't want to leave her.

So, in May 2003, the three men had set off on a

perfect autumn day to spend an entire week in the Rockhampton and Yeppoon area. While most of the break was to be cattle and farm related, they had also booked a fishing trip which Robert had been looking forward to.

But the plane never arrived at its destination. Hours after they left the Dalgonally airstrip, Lucy had received the shocking news that the aircraft had gone down in bush southwest of their goal. There were no survivors.

The rest of the year had passed in a thick fog for Lucy. Adam had been distraught. His schoolwork suffered, and he barely slept for weeks. It had been Matthew who had taken him under his wing, and eventually a more serious, mature Adam had emerged. By the time the 2004 school year began, Adam and his cousin, Nick, had settled into their new life with purpose. They would be the next managers of Dalgonally and to succeed in making it one of the most productive properties in the area, they needed to achieve good results in their education and move on to completing higher studies in the agricultural industry.

Finally, Lucy had been able to grieve. Not only for the gentle, caring man she had lived with for almost twelve years, but also for her beloved father.

Her mouth twitched in a wry smile as she walked past the workshop where Brent had mended damaged equipment, created nesting boxes to fix to trees for the wild birds, and shaped hundreds of wire outriggers to support the electric fences. A sign sat in the corner, drawing her eye to the faded name. Now coated with cobwebs and wasps' nests, it had proudly stood next to their mailbox before the mail run had been rerouted to omit their little side road and include only the highway. When it grew shabby, Brent had removed it, planning to sand it back and repaint the name "Binnalong" on it. But that had never happened as Dalgonally and Binnalong had become one encompassing property again, exactly as it had been two generations earlier.

She moved on before stopping and sitting on the veranda of her father's cabin. Following his death, it had sat idle for over a year. Then with Adam and his cousins away at boarding school—with the exception of the two baby girls, Ivy and Ella—Matthew, Kylie, Belinda, and Lucy had gathered for a much overdue business meeting and her life had once again changed dramatically.

After having a list of advantages repeatedly hammered into her by the Venables family—who Lucy had long ago realised arguing with was pointless—she had agreed to allow Matthew to sharefarm the majority of Binnalong. This would mean that while the land would still remain hers, Matthew would take over the cattle and cropping portion and pay Lucy forty per cent of the annual profits. The Dalgonally family business, of which she had fiercely stayed independent from, would retain the balance.

After the drought finally broke in 1996, farming Binnalong had become a pleasure. Both crops and cattle had grown fat, and the years of hardship gradually peeled away as profits increased. But by the time Adam was five and started school, Lucy and her father had mutually agreed it would be good for her to return to nursing.

The aged care home she had previously enjoyed working in welcomed her back and she looked forward to the two days each week that she drove into Roma to care for those who could no longer care for themselves. While most of her memory gaps had gradually been filled, a few pieces of the year leading up to her accident remained missing.

One of those gaps was her months in Scotland, of which she remembered nothing.

Lucy rose to her feet and returned to the house, Jet trotting faithfully at her side, and with each step, her resolve deepened. She glanced around before adding a skip to her stride, as though demonstrating her excitement as a woman approaching sixty instead of six might not be allowed.

After Brent's death, it had taken months before

Lucy could clear her father's belongings from the cabin. Then, with Kylie's encouragement, she had rented it out on a regular basis for farmstay accommodation. Together with her nursing income and the small business she had set up supplying the florist shops in town with native flowers and foliage suitable for arrangements from her growing plantation, the farmstay had ensured she and Adam had managed financially, without having to touch the bonus from the sharefarming arrangement. That, she had squirreled away for boarding school fees—and potentially university expenses if Adam needed them.

She made herself a pot of tea and sat at the kitchen table to drink it. The pile of mail on the side bench caught her eye and she groaned.

'I suppose I had better sort that out to begin with—and then think about what I want to take to the cabin,' she said to Jet, who was on the veranda, leaning against the screen door as if hoping it might magically open and let him inside to be closer to his favourite person.

The decision to move to the cabin had been hers. It was perfectly roomy enough for one—a good-sized bedroom, a smaller room she would use as her study, a combined living/kitchen/dining room, and a bathroom. Her father had continued to use the homestead laundry—and had joined them for every evening meal and most lunches while he lived there. Now it was her turn to vacate the homestead for Adam and Meg, and give them the privacy her father had afforded her and Robert.

They had mutually agreed the furniture would remain. She would take only the items she cherished. A tea set that had been her grandmother's, a beautiful dinner set with hydrangeas around the edges Adam had bought her for her fiftieth birthday, and the baking equipment she used every week to fill the tins with Adam's favourites and now those of Meg—Anzac biscuits, cheese straws, and chocolate cake. Most of the coffee cups were heavy and some had chips, so she would treat herself to a new set.

Other than that, she would take what linen she needed and her clothes and books. Everything else would allow the young couple a good start without having to buy a thing.

Her stomach fluttered as she considered the one area she hadn't touched for decades—her old bedroom. Except for a regular vacuum and dust, it was the only room no one went into except on the rare occasions that Mandy visited and stayed overnight— and that was never more than once a year. When she did stay, any garments requiring a hanger were hooked to the wardrobe door and other than that, she dived into her overnight bag, seemingly unwilling to unpack it properly in case it indicated she was staying longer.

Having slept in the same bed in the same room her entire childhood—and for the few months after her overseas holiday before she married Robert—for some reason Lucy had been reluctant to share it. Before her parents had added their bedroom and ensuite to the compact home, the two girls had shared the tiny room. But once the alterations were made, Mandy had quickly moved into what had been her parents' room —and was now Adam's.

Lucy pushed her chair back and rinsed her mug in the sink. 'It's not going to clear itself out, is it my friend?' she said, glancing at Jet. 'This could be quite an experience—and a walk down memory lane.'

Chuckling at her own reference to memories, she strode down the hall and into the room before she could change her mind.

30

An hour later, she sat on the floor, surrounded by old schoolbooks, reports, photographs, and birthday cards dating back more than fifty years. Muttering as she read each item, she sorted everything into piles—one to burn, one to return to the old suitcase and shove back under the bed for Adam and Meg to deal with if and when they chose to, and one to keep and reread after she moved before deciding what their destination would be.

After clearing the floorspace, she opened the wardrobe. A fusty, floral scent greeted her—the old-world fragrance of long-dead lavender bags and camphor packets.

There were no longer any clothes hanging from the narrow rail. She had moved them into her parents' bedroom after she and Robert had married and her father shifted into the cabin. Instead, the cupboard had become a storage area for disused suitcases, old hats, and handbags whose acrylic coating had disintegrated into colourful flakes that drifted out to greet her.

She sneezed as dust motes floated around her and looked despairingly at the growing pile overflowing into the hallway. Then she opened the largest of the suitcases and after systematically checking each bag in case of forgotten treasures hidden inside, she dumped them all into it. One or two of the travel bags were still in good condition, so she put them on the bed before carrying everything else out to the veranda. These she would deal with later—most likely on her next trip to Roma when she would stop first at the town waste facility.

Back in the bedroom, she vacuumed up the dust and debris scattered on the floor then moved to the cupboard to wipe the top shelf and give the corners a final check for insects and other unexpected surprises.

Reaching up on her tiptoes, she swept the damp cloth along the shelf, surprised when her skin encountered the edge of a box. She pulled it toward her, astonished to see there were two boxes, one on top of the other. Dropping the rag on the floor behind her, she carefully lifted them down and placed them on the desktop. Flicking the lid off the top box, she smiled at the shoes—now dated despite their pristine condition.

Moving it to the side, she stared at the second box, her eyes fixed on it for a long minute.

Slowly, as though uncoiling an ancient roll of movie tape, the recollection of a young girl gluing left-over wrapping paper onto an old shoebox trickled back. She was sitting at the table, her mother peeling vegetables.

Goosebumps tickled her arms as the intense rush of emotion jammed in her throat.

'My writing box,' she whispered.

She removed the lid, her forehead creasing as she lifted out the wad of pale blue letters. Setting them to the side, she continued to unpack the box. Cards, pens, stamps, and blank envelopes fell out on the desk, a vaguely familiar gold chain, the final item.

Picking up the letters, she sat, sifting through them one by one.

There were eight altogether—all from the same person.

Her breath caught in her throat as nerves fluttered to life in her belly.

Glancing at the one in her hand, she turned it over and read the sender's name and address again.

Fergus MacRae

Ardvasar Post Office

Isle of Skye

Scotland

Who was Fergus MacRae? She read on.

Dear Lucy,

I didn't get a letter from you last week, or this, so I hope you're alright. I know life on a farm gets busy and you and your dad will still be grieving for your mother, so I suppose that's it.

The wind has been wild these past weeks and I've kept the fire going night and day. Winter is here, so we've begun feeding the sheep and will have to bring them in if the weather worsens. The tups (or rams as you call them) are out with the ewes now—they seem happy! Christmas is around the corner. I had hoped you'd be back for your first Skye winter but there'll be more opportunities.

I don't know what else to say. Life can feel very empty after losing someone you love. I felt that way when my grandfather died and can only imagine how hard it is losing a beloved mother. I'm thinking of you though and sending my love.

I look forward to receiving your news.

All my love,

F xx

Lucy re-read the words twice before folding the letter and placing it to the side. Inspecting each postal date on the others, she put them in order and began reading.

An hour went by, then another. She read every letter several times over before clutching the final, brief one in her hands as she read it again.

My darling Lucy,

I don't know what has happened or why your letters aren't reaching me. I've been to the post office and enquired but Moira couldn't help.

I can only assume you have changed your mind about us and our future together. Unless something awful has happened—and I can't bear to think about that.

If I don't receive your reply to this letter, I won't write again. But I will wait—forever if I have to—until we meet again.

And I will always love you.

Fergus xx

Her head swam with confusion, her eyes glistening with unshed tears.

'Love letters,' she whispered. 'These are love letters from someone called Fergus—and they're all addressed to me.'

LUCY LAY FOR HOURS, moving only when the whine of her impatient dog reached her ears.

Pushing herself to her feet, she stumbled to the kitchen. A cold wind filtered through the screen door, and she shivered.

'Come inside, Jet,' she said, pushing it open.

The dog headed straight to the thick cushion-bed beside the range.

Opening the fire box, Lucy grunted. The flickering

glow of a blackened piece of charcoal was all that was left. She looked up at the clock, switched on the light, and glanced through the window.

Where had the afternoon gone? The light was fading—cold, grey clouds scudding across the sky, highlighting the rolling hills in shades of purple and olive green.

'Good grief,' she said aloud. 'I haven't done a thing outside!'

She stoked the fire, placing one piece of wood at a time on the pile. Leaving the door ajar, she continued to feed the stove until flames licked the walls of the firebox and heat began to once again radiate toward her. She closed and latched the little door and turned to face Jet, her head fuzzy with the effort of separating the whirl of mystery from the chores that had to be done.

'I suppose we'd better see to the chooks and pick veggies for dinner.'

The two of them drifted outside, completed the tasks, and hurried back into the gradually warming kitchen.

In a daze, she removed a bowl of mince from the fridge and tipped it into a saucepan. Then she proceeded to chop up vegetables and added them together with a liberal dose of herbs. She had no idea what she was creating, but years of instinct guided her while the little voice in her head repeated the name again and again.

'Fergus MacRae, Fergus MacRae.'

WITH THE TELEVISION talking to itself after dinner, Lucy lay on the couch, listening to the wind howling in the trees surrounding the house yard, recalling every word written on those thin blue sheets of paper.

She must have dozed off, comforted by the fire's warmth and the knowledge that Jet was asleep on his indoor bed. Except for the years when Adam was at boarding school and university, she had rarely been alone. Matthew and Kylie visited regularly, often bringing extra workers to assist with farm jobs. Her kitchen was filled with hungry adults and children and during school and university holidays, her house felt chaotic—which didn't bother her one bit.

She sat up, the image powering through her as if driven by an electric current.

His face was in front of hers, smiling, his blue eyes twinkling with mirth. In an instant, she knew it wasn't Robert even though the colour of their eyes was similar. But this face was rounder, the eyebrows thick and black, and with a dark, shadowed jaw.

'Fergus?'

The image faded but the memory remained ...

broadened until the vision of a white-painted croft surrounded by daffodils and green fields dotted with purple-flowing heather washed in.

Little by little, snippets returned, sparking her brain into a jumble of pictures not unlike the suitcase of photos she'd unearthed from her wardrobe earlier that day. Only these were of the sea lapping the shore, the darkened smudge of the mainland across the Sound. Boats nudged the timber pylons, and on the hills and gullies surrounding a small Scottish village, the sound of bleating sheep drifted in the air.

The Isle of Skye!

Memories rolled in—broken in tiny pieces like a confusing thousand-piece jigsaw.

She slumped back onto the cushions, her eyes wide as she stared at the ceiling.

I had a whole other life!

31

Queensland, July 2024 – Ingrid

INGRID SCUTTLED out the hospital door, checking her watch as she hurried. She had exactly four minutes before her break was over—just enough time to send Callum a message.

Grabbing her phone, the second she reached the fresh air, she tapped rapidly on the screen.

Guess what! Pure coincidence, Lucy's sister came into this hospital to visit someone. She wore a name tag, so I asked her if she knew Lucy. Can't believe our luck. Long story short—Lucy's alive and still living on Binnalong, except it's not called Binnalong anymore. Will ring you tonight. XX

She hit send and hurried back to the emergency department. The remainder of her shift passed slowly, her concentration scattered. Fighting to keep her mind on her work, Ingrid breathed a sigh of relief when her substitute arrived. She exchanged notes, grabbed her jacket and bag, and ran to her car.

Mandy Pellegreen hadn't exchanged exact details about Lucy's whereabouts but now Ingrid had confirmation she still lived on Dalgonally.

The trip home seemed to take forever. Every set of lights turned red as she reached it and even though she wouldn't call Callum until she was certain he would be awake—a delay of almost three hours—she drummed her fingers impatiently on the steering wheel.

'Hey, Mum.' She greeted Vonnie with an exuberant hug as she kicked the door shut behind her. 'You'll never guess what happened at work today,' she breathed.

'Tell me.'

Ingrid dropped her bag on the couch and flung herself down beside it. 'I met Lucy Pellegreen's sister!'

Vonnie raised an eyebrow. 'Really? THE Lucy Pellegreen you've been looking for?'

'Yes. Well, not Lucy. As I said, I met her sister at work—she was visiting someone and had her name badge on. As soon as I saw the surname I asked if she knew Lucy.'

Ingrid continued to share the afternoon's discovery, finishing with a jubilant release of breath.

'So, what do you reckon? I've got an early shift tomorrow. If we get organised this evening, we could drive out there after work and visit Lucy on Sunday—if it suits her of course.'

'Well,' Vonnie drawled. 'I suppose so—if Lucy is prepared to talk to you. She doesn't know you. How are you going to broach the subject over the phone?'

'Hmm. Good point.' Ingrid bounced to her feet again. 'I'm getting changed then going for a run. That'll clear my head and when I return, we'll have dinner then I'll call the number on the website—and Callum.'

THE PHONE RANG for so long Ingrid was about to disconnect when a woman answered.

'Dalgonally. Kylie speaking.'

'Hello, Kylie. My name is Ingrid Sloane. I've been speaking with Mandy Pellegreen today and would like to talk to her sister please—Cindy Venables.'

'Oh.' There was a slight pause. 'Cindy doesn't live here. She's on another part of the property. I'll give you her number.'

She shared the details and ended the call.

Ingrid drew a deep breath and punched the number into her phone.

Disappointment burned in Ingrid's chest as the call rang out with no opportunity to leave a message.

'Blast,' she growled. 'Oh well, at least I have her number. I'll ring Callum instead.'

'Any luck?' her mother called.

'No answer. I'm ringing Callum and will tell him the news. Then I'll try her again later.'

'Okay.' The door between the lounge and Ingrid's room closed.

Ingrid smiled, gratitude warming her. Her mother had always been understanding and respected Ingrid's privacy as much as she valued her own.

Seconds later, Callum's voice boomed through the phone as though he was in the next room.

'Hi there!'

'Hi.' She made herself more comfortable, her smile widening. 'Did you get my message?'

'Sure did. You clever girl. Tell me all about it.'

They talked for over an hour, sharing the excitement of Ingrid's meeting with Mandy before continuing with Callum's less riveting day and the latest interaction with Fergus.

'We're supposed to be making silage today. What will I tell him? Should I mention you've found Lucy? That she's alive?'

'Of course. Until I talk to her, I don't have any more information—but it would be interesting to see his reaction once he knows she's fine and, from the little Mandy shared, single again.'

She chuckled, buoyed by the success of her sleuthing—together with an unbelievable stroke of good luck. The vision of lush, green paddocks filled with grasses ripe for harvesting filled her senses. She could almost smell the fresh sea air and newly mown vegetation. Glancing down at her watch, she groaned.

'Bother. I don't know how we managed to talk so long. It's nearly nine o'clock here—too late for me to try her number again tonight.'

His deep, caring tone soothed her annoyance in an instant.

'Don't panic. There's always tomorrow—and I can let you know how I get on with Fergus today.' He laughed quietly. 'You're nearly there, Sherlock.'

Her chest fluttered with a mixture of relief and elation. 'We are, Watson.'

32

———

 *ueensland, July 2024 – Mandy*

MANDY'S HEAD SPUN, her stomach gripped with pain. Not the pain of having eaten the wrong thing or suffering with a gastric virus. This was panic. Guilt. Anguish. She drained the water cup then, glancing around to ensure she was alone, she leaned forward, resting her elbows on her knees.

What have I done?

It took several minutes to regain control, by which time she had made her plan. She would check on her colleague then, instead of returning to Brisbane, she would continue westward for another four hours to see Lucy.

Her sister would be surprised, shocked even. Mandy never did things on the "spur of the moment". She was a planner and any visits to her old home were always pre-arranged. Now, there was no time.

Horror gripped her as she considered the possibility of Ingrid finding Lucy before she had a chance to speak to her first. Then she relaxed a little, reassuring herself her sister probably wouldn't believe Ingrid, even if she did fly out to Roma in the next few days. She had no memory of Fergus and, hopefully no memory of those blue letters that Mandy had shoved away all those years ago, convinced she was doing the right thing by not upsetting Lucy further. After all, her sister had been in no state to leave the country and if she couldn't remember anything of the previous few months, there was no harm in saving her the anguish of wanting to return to the Isle of Skye but being too unwell to do so.

With the setting sun flashing through the windscreen as she drove, Mandy pulled gratefully into the servo in Chinchilla. A toasted sandwich and coffee would see her through the rest of the journey, and by the time she had consumed them, the sun would have set.

Kangaroos! Mandy grimaced. For decades, she had avoided driving on country roads in the early morning or around dusk to evade interaction with the skittish creatures that ridiculously chose to flock to the edges of the road to graze at those specific times of the day. Not to mention hopping from one side to the other, often in groups as though determined to have at least one of their mob collide with an oncoming vehicle.

She huffed as she waited. There was no choice but to drive slower than she usually did if she wanted to reach Dalgonally in one piece.

IT WAS after nine o'clock when she drove along the familiar gravelled road leading to the home she'd grown up in.

A light shone through the kitchen window, illuminating the neat lawn and even neater garden. A dog barked as she drew nearer. Within seconds, the veranda lit up. Mandy braked in front of the house gate and got out of the car, pulling her jacket more tightly around her. Breathing out white, foggy breath in the cold, still air, she approached with uneasy caution.

'Mandy! What are you doing here?'

'Hi, Lucy. Sorry I didn't ring.' She stopped, hesitating at the foot of the steps. 'I need to talk to you—and I didn't want to do it over the phone.'

Lucy clutched the top of her jumper as if the thick, fleecy fabric was attempting to choke her. 'What's happened?' Her face paled. 'Have you got bad news?'

Mandy shivered. 'God, it's freezing out here and I'm

tired. I came straight from Toowoomba where I was visiting a colleague in hospital. I haven't even got a change of clothes.' Her voice was more desperate than she'd intended.

Lucy reached for her and folded her in a hug. 'Come in and I'll put the kettle on. Adam and Meg are away at a campdrafting competition for the weekend, so it's just Jet and me here.'

For the next few minutes, the sisters dealt with practicalities as though dancing around the reason for Mandy's arrival, too terrified to share or receive the news. With the essential visit to the bathroom and the exchange of shoes for a spare pair of slippers for Mandy complete, they sat on the couch, each clutching a mug of tea and a chocolate biscuit.

'RIGHT,' Lucy said. 'Tell me what's bothering you.'

'It's about the Isle of Skye,' Mandy blurted.

Lucy coughed, almost choking on her biscuit. 'Really? I've been cleaning out my old bedroom today and I found the box I used to keep my treasures in. You remember, that one I covered with different-patterned paper and you thought it looked hideous.'

Mandy froze.

'I found letters from a man called Fergus. I was going to call you to see if you could help solve the mystery, but I needed to get my head around everything first—and I'm still not quite sure if I've managed to achieve that.'

After placing her mug on the coffee table, Mandy met Lucy's stare. 'Are you telling me you remember him?'

'I think so. I think we were lovers,' she whispered.

'Oh, Lucy. I'm so sorry.'

'What are you sorry about?'

'After you had your accident, before you were discharged from hospital, I came out and gave the house a good clean.'

Lucy rolled her eyes. 'You've never considered my housekeeping up to standard, but I don't hold that against you'. She grinned and continued, 'I try to keep the house spick and span, but you have to accept that living in the middle of a working farm inevitably brings dust, dirt, and flies. And while this house can't compare with your smart townhouse on the coast, it has loads of character. I imagine salt air and the smell of traffic filtering through the windows is about the worst you have to contend with?'

Mandy gave a hoot of laughter. 'You're right.' She interlaced her fingers and studied them. 'Anyway. As I was saying, I cleaned the house and tidied your room to make it more welcoming for you when you got home.' Her lip quivered unexpectedly. 'I never dreamed that you wouldn't remember Fergus—or forget you ever had that box. As time went by and your memory didn't return, I was more worried about you and Dad. Then you and Robert married, and I forgot about the letters. I never thought about your holiday on the Isle of Skye at all—until I met Ingrid this afternoon.'

Lucy frowned. 'Who's Ingrid?'

'A nurse at the Toowoomba hospital. Apparently, she's been looking for you—even drove out here to see if she could track you down.' She continued to explain the interaction between herself and Ingrid earlier in the afternoon, finishing as Lucy slumped back into the couch, her hand on her mouth.

Neither woman spoke for several minutes. Then Mandy leaned forward, adding, 'Are you telling me this is the first time you've cleaned out that cupboard in thirty-four years?'

Lucy drew a deep breath and nodded, sharing a rueful grin. 'Yes. It's ironic that you're here.' She glanced up at the ceiling. 'Mum again?' She shrugged at Mandy's snort, continuing as if she hadn't noticed her sister's reaction. 'My sub-standard housekeeping aside—and because I've decided to move to the cabin and let Adam and Meg have this house to themselves —I remembered my old bedroom needed repainting. I'm not sure why it wasn't done when we did the rest of the house, but I think it had something to do with rain arriving at the right time, so planting got in the way.'

She shot Mandy a wry smile. 'Anyway, I got rid of stuff I didn't know was still there—and as I said, I found the letters.'

'I think I need another cup of tea,' Mandy said.

Lucy filled the kettle while Mandy rummaged through the pantry.

'Have you got any crackers? I feel like something savoury.' She glanced at her sister's wiry body. 'It's alright for you to munch on chocolate biscuits but if I do more than smell them, I'm guaranteed to gain a kilo!'

They laughed—a relaxed, happy, impulsive laugh that Mandy couldn't remember sharing in a long, long time.

'I need to get out of this suit,' Mandy said. 'Have you got anything I can borrow?'

'Sure. You make the tea and I'll hunt something up for you. You'll have to sleep in my old room tonight. I promise you'll approve, even if the painting won't be getting done this weekend.'

Chuckling, Lucy left the room.

Mandy poured the tea, the weight of her confession sliding off her shoulders.

33

Queensland, July 2024 – Lucy

LEAVING Mandy to enjoy a sleep in—at least until the frost thawed and she had the fire raging, Lucy had fed the chooks and was entering the house again when the phone rang.

She placed the eggs carefully on the bench and answered. 'Hello?'

'Hello. Is that Lucy?'

A lump of dread jammed in her throat. She swallowed it and drew a deep breath.

'Cindy Venables, also known as Lucy Venables. Yes, it is me.'

A whoosh of relieved breath sounded down the phone before the woman continued. 'My name is Ingrid Sloane. You don't know me, but I met your sister, Mandy, yesterday and I wondered if you could spare a few minutes to talk with me?'

Lucy's heart thumped so hard she pressed a hand against her chest before she answered, fearful the heartbeats would be heard by her caller. She drew a long breath in an attempt to still it.

'Are you still there?' Ingrid asked.

'Yes. I'm here. My sister is with me too.' She turned at the sound of slippers scuffing the timber floor.

'Is it her?' Mandy mouthed.

Lucy nodded. 'I think I know what this conversation is about. Do you mind if I put you on speaker?'

'No,' Ingrid said. 'That's fine.'

Lucy pushed the button and lay the phone on the table between Mandy and herself. 'Go ahead then, Ingrid.'

'I ... I'm not really sure where to begin.'

Recognising the nervous hesitation in the young woman's voice, a sudden calm washed over Lucy. She made herself comfortable in the chair and smiled at Mandy as she spoke. 'My sister has mentioned you have a friend who has been trying to find me. Is that correct?'

'Yes. It is. It seems you and he were ... a couple

about thirty-four years ago. I met him when holidaying on the Isle of Skye recently and he mentioned you.'

'I see. Go on.'

'He tried to find you apparently, but I guess he didn't exactly have the sleuthing techniques required.' A faint chuckle sounded. 'Anyway, Callum, his nephew, and I realised how much he thinks about you so decided to help—and here we are.'

'Thank you, Ingrid. No doubt you had a problem due to my name change. I understand. But to put you at ease, I really can't tell you whether I'm pleased to hear you've now found me or not.'

A momentary pause. 'Why?' Ingrid asked.

Before Lucy had a chance to gather her thoughts and form a feasible answer, Ingrid continued.

'Would it be possible to talk face to face? I have a lot to tell you and it doesn't seem right discussing it over the phone. Also, I'm at work and my morning break is almost over.'

Lucy glanced at Mandy, who shrugged.

It took only a second for Lucy to decide. 'Of course. Would you like to meet somewhere—or come to my home?'

'Oh! Thank you. My mother and I had planned a road trip out your way over the next couple of days. Would it suit for us to visit your home tomorrow afternoon?'

Lucy's eyes widened in question as she met Mandy's gaze. 'Yes. That would be perfect.'

She shared the exact details of how to reach the house before they said goodbye and ended the call.

Questions batted around in her mind like a moth against a window, while surprisingly, a sense of calm, of déjà vu swept through her body.

'Do I really want to do this? Or have I just opened a can of worms?'

'Well,' Mandy said kindly, 'you'll never know unless you hear what Ingrid has to say.'

Lucy nodded, a surge of excited anticipation filling her. She rose and filled the kettle.

'I wish I could stay—or at least be a fly on the wall,' Mandy said as she hugged Lucy.

'I wish you could too, but I know you've got a long journey home and a busy week coming up. I'll ring you tonight—before Adam and Meg get back and update you.'

'Perfect.'

Lucy stepped back and they shared a smile as a tingle of happiness swelled.

Mandy slid into her car and moved off, giving a toot of the horn and waving madly through the open window as the vehicle disappeared down the track.

Lucy remained stationary, Jet sitting alert and questioning at her feet until long after the dust had settled.

It had been a weekend of revelations. Old memories, once triggered, trickled back like a slow stream, joined by an occasional rush of clarity. A vision of the Ardvasar Hotel began, evolving into the village with its neat cottages dotted along the roadside. The lane leading to a solid, white croft surrounded by colours of the rainbow followed. Purple heather, green pastures, yellow broom, and bluebells spread like a blanket over the land. And a broad, dark-haired man with the bluest eyes she'd ever seen smiled at her.

Her heart leapt. She had loved that man. Years had passed and she had been oblivious to his existence. Her lost love—and her lost memory.

A sob caught in her throat and for a moment, she wanted to slump into the dust and bawl her eyes out. Instead, she swung her gaze around the farm. Her farm —well, hers and Adam's. The small but well-maintained homestead, it's white paint and steel roof glinting in the winter sunshine, surrounded by garden beds and shrubs. Paddocks a colourful patchwork of bright green barley, rows of native trees, their olive-green leaves swishing in the breeze, and the contrasting honey-coloured stalks, remnants of the sorghum crop harvested weeks earlier.

She drew a deep, shuddering breath and dropped her shoulders. Life had certainly dealt some ups and downs, but she was happy here, despite having experienced the loss of loved ones.

Her insides fluttered, her face softening. In less than two hours, Ingrid would be here. She would make a cake and perhaps a batch of shortbread for afternoon tea. That would acknowledge the discussion she presumed was going to occur—life in Scotland.

34

———————

The small, white car approached slowly, drawing up outside the yard gate.

Jet yipped, his call summoning Lucy from the kitchen.

She wiped her hands on the towel and cast a quick glance at the table. Her best cloth, her grandmother's dainty tea set with its blue forget-me-nots decorating the fine bone china, and a smorgasbord of home baking, crackers and cheese, and in the centre, a fruit platter. Perhaps a touch overdone, but it wasn't often she entertained two women who appeared to be on a revelation-filled mission. Besides, she had needed something to keep herself busy while the time ticked by exasperatingly slowly.

An attractive young woman with a long, blonde ponytail stepped out, immediately followed by a smaller woman of around Lucy's own age who stood, one hand on the car's roof, as she straightened her back. Undoubtedly Ingrid's mother. Lucy smiled at them both, noting the older woman's stylishly cut fair hair and perfectly matching slacks and jumper, a vibrant-coloured scarf loosely knotted around her neck. She ran a hand down her well-worn jeans and wished she'd changed into a smarter top.

'Hello, Lucy. I'm Ingrid.' The younger woman reached out a hand, and Lucy took it before squeezing it gently.

'Hello there. Welcome to Dalgonally.' Lucy's gaze switched to the older woman as she reached them both.

'And I'm Vonnie, Ingrid's mother. I hope you don't mind me imposing on you, only Ingrid thought it would be nice for us to have a road trip together.'

'Of course not. I agree. How lovely for you both.'

She waved toward the house. 'Will you come in?'

They trooped inside, Lucy dismissing Ingrid and Vonnie's attempt at removing their shoes.

'Please, leave them on. It's winter and although the fire is burning, the floor can be cold.'

Further pleasantries filled the next few minutes as Lucy led them into the lounge and they sat, staring at each other.

Lucy drew a deep breath. 'I'm not sure where we should begin really, but before you share your side of things, Ingrid, I would like to explain why I didn't return to Skye—and why I failed to contact Fergus.'

A magpie warbled outside the room as if to signal it was time to reveal all.

Lucy began with the phone call from Mandy summoning her home before explaining the accident, her loss of memory, her marriage and subsequent widowhood, and lastly, her current, incredibly unbelievable weekend.

'I'm not sure why or how I missed cleaning out that cupboard, but, in the way those odd coincidences occur, it was obviously meant to be as within hours of me finding those aerogrammes, Ingrid met Mandy who stayed last night and told me everything. It seems that while I was in hospital all those years ago, she tidied my room—she was always a bit fanatical and I was such an outdoor girl, my housekeeping happily omitted chores like cleaning out cupboards in rooms that were rarely used.'

Ingrid grinned at her before glancing at her mother. 'I understand. I'm not the greatest organiser, am I, Mum?'

Vonnie returned the smile. 'You weren't as a teenager but since you've moved home again, I'm delighted to disagree.'

'So, you live together?' Lucy asked.

'Yes,' Vonnie said. 'About a year ago, Tony, my husband, developed dementia and as he deteriorated,

Ingrid felt I needed help. She had purchased her own two-bedroom unit. However, I'm very grateful she rented it out and moved back in with us as I'm not sure I could have coped with him at home for so long on my own. He passed away a few weeks ago.'

'I'm sorry to hear of your loss. I, too, lost my husband—more than twenty years ago now, but I have a son, Adam, who lives here with his fiancée and runs the farm. They're away at a campdraft competition this weekend and should be home tonight.'

Lucy's download surprised her, uncertain why it seemed so easy to talk to two women she'd never heard of before yesterday. But something about them felt comfortable—more like old friends or relations.

She shuffled forward in her seat. 'Your turn now, Ingrid. Please tell me how you and Fergus met?'

It took only minutes for Ingrid to share her side of the story. Then she withdrew her phone from her pocket. 'Callum sent me a photo he found of the two of you. Would you like to see it?'

With trepidation, Lucy took the phone from Ingrid's outstretched hand and bowed her head to study the picture. Although slightly pixelated and blurred, the memory returned to her as though it had been yesterday. They stood outside the croft—a tall, solid man in farm clothes with his arm wrapped tightly around a slim, brown-haired girl looking up at him adoringly.

She touched her mouth with her palm, her breath tight in her chest and her whole body consumed with an unfamiliar ache.

'It's us. Fergus and me.'

'Yes, and if you swipe across, you'll see a close up of Fergus.'

She followed Ingrid's instructions, her back rigid as she stared into eyes that had haunted her for decades. Initially she'd believed they were Robert's, but now she knew. They had always been Fergus's—and he had been the one she loved.

As though suddenly released from a corked bottle of champagne, memories came tumbling back. Not only the croft, but happy afternoons out picking black-berries in summer, shearing sheep, hiking in the Cuillin Mountains, and their stolen nights together in her staff bedroom at the hotel.

'Let's have afternoon tea,' Lucy said. 'I'm parched. Then you can tell me more about Fergus. How is he? What does he look like?'

Ingrid laughed. 'Sounds lovely. How can I help?'

ANOTHER HOUR PASSED as they ate, drank a pot of tea, and Ingrid shared her holiday, her blossoming friend-ship with Callum, and her desire to return to the Isle of Skye.

For the first time in her adult life, Lucy likened her feelings to an onion. She laughed as she described them. 'Hearing all this is incredible. For years, there have been gaps in my memory. Some I may never get back, but mostly I have felt normal and been able to live a good life. But the period leading up to my accident was the one era I just couldn't remember. Now, since meeting you and hearing Mandy's side of things too, it feels as though layers of me have been peeled back, one at a time. Only now, I have no idea what I should do.'

35

As the pale winter sunshine began to fade, Lucy reluctantly farewelled Ingrid and Vonnie, having agreed to meet them in Toowoomba the following week.

In the hours between their departure and Adam and Meg's homecoming, she digested all that had transpired over the weekend, assembled the facts, and temporarily ignored the emotions they stirred. Now she faced her son and soon-to-be daughter-in-law and announced the news she had waited thirty-four years for.

'While you've been away, something happened.'

A cloud crossed Adam's face and he stilled. 'No.'

She lay a reassuring hand on his arm and smiled. 'It's a long story, but it seems a missing piece of my memory has returned. I think the amnesia has finally healed. I'm back to my old self—at least as much as I can be after all these years.'

'Are you serious, Mum? How?' Adam said, his voice filled with relief and high-pitched with incredulity.

'Sit down. This might take a while.'

They did as she bid, organising themselves around the kitchen table.

She began by collecting the aerogrammes from the sideboard and placing them in front of them.

'What are these?' Meg asked.

'The link to my past—and the unearthing of a whole different life.'

Adam's forehead creased in confusion. He opened his mouth and closed it again.

Beginning with her overseas holiday in 1990, Lucy unravelled the years. Neither Adam nor Meg said a word, their gazes glued to hers as though she was revealing her experience of a trip into space a hundred years earlier.

She ended with the discovery of the aerogrammes, her weekend visitors including Mandy's confessions, and finally the extraordinary connection with Ingrid and the Isle of Skye.

Meg's eyes glistened with unshed tears, Adam rocked back in his chair, and silence filled the air.

'What a beautiful—and sad story.' Meg finally spoke. Like Lucy, she was a romance reader and had, in the two years she and Adam had been together, progressed her way through Lucy's shelves of Mills and Boon novels before switching to reading eBooks on her tablet.

'It's amazing, Mum.' Adam leaned forward and placed his hand on hers. 'Not only the return of those missing bits in your memory, but all that stuff about being in Scotland! Who knew those aerogrammes would change so much?'

The band gripping her insides eased a notch. She had been terrified he might have suggested she had double-crossed Robert—or worse still, somehow tricked Robert into marrying her under false pretences.

But he didn't. Instead, his sapphire gaze bored into hers.

'You're worried we might think you lied to Dad. Kept secrets he had a right to know,' he said.

She nodded and allowed a tear to escape. 'I didn't know any of this when we married. I'm not sure what would have happened if I'd discovered the aerogrammes while he was still alive. But that didn't happen and I promise you, I had no memory of that year and I knew your father and I could make a good life together.'

'It's okay, Mum. I believe you. I wouldn't be here if you hadn't got together. And I reckon Dad would be delighted to know you're happy, even if there was another fella in your life before him,' he finished with a cheeky smile.

'I think we need a cup of tea,' Meg said, jumping up and filling the kettle.

'So what are you thinking, Mum. Are you going to contact this guy?'

She drew a long breath. 'Not sure. I wanted to tell you both first. I've agreed to meet Ingrid and her mother in Toowoomba sometime in the next few days. Ingrid is in contact with Fergus's nephew. Actually, I think there might be a budding romance there too.' She smiled. 'He's been finding old photos and sending them to her, and it seems they talk or message regularly. I'm not sure where things will go now they've found me, but I do want to talk with them more—and Ingrid suggested if I would like to stay overnight in Toowoomba, we could talk to him via video in the evening when it's early morning in Scotland.'

Meg placed a mug of tea in front of each of them. 'Do you want to reconnect with this Fergus guy?'

Lucy wrapped her hands around the mug. 'To be honest, I really don't know.' Her shoulders slumped. 'There's so much to take in. And it all happened so long ago. What if he's a grumpy old guy with missing teeth and a pot belly?'

Both Adam and Meg hooted with laughter.

'When he hears you're alive and kicking, he'll probably be thinking the same about you,' Adam said.

Lucy grimaced. 'You're right. I can't imagine he would have changed much. He was that type of build that seems to age gracefully, and when we were young, he could have afforded a bit of extra meat on his bones.'

She stood and studied herself in the window, turning her head one way then the other. 'Do I look old and crabby?'

'Mum. You're approaching sixty. You can't expect to look like you did back then—what age were you? Twenty something?'

'I was twenty-four,' she breathed. 'And I thought I had the world at my feet.'

Meg hugged her, touching a strand of Lucy's hair. 'You still look very young for your age—slim, active, and with hardly any greys.'

'Thank you.' Lucy grinned. 'Like that old saying, I suppose it's all in the eyes of the beholder.'

Buoyed by Adam and Meg's confident acceptance of her situation, Lucy phoned Vonnie the next morning and arranged to drive to Toowoomba on Wednesday. Ingrid's scheduled shifts on both days were six forty-five until three in the afternoon, which would allow them ample time to talk, enjoy dinner together, and share a video call with Callum.

Lucy wasn't sure how she felt about that. The thought of her past springing to life again in the form of a man who, according to Ingrid, was a younger version of his uncle, both terrified and exhilarated her.

Stop being silly. You've got nothing to lose. Connecting with old friends is a good thing—isn't it?

Before she could change her mind, she grabbed her little-used overnight bag from the cupboard and began assembling clothes and toiletries.

It seemed ridiculous but she couldn't help herself. Butterflies created havoc in her stomach as she carefully pushed her well-worn garments aside and selected an elegant cream cashmere jumper and an autumn-toned silk scarf. She would wash and blow-dry her hair on Wednesday morning, treating it to a dose of the bonus "extra-gloss" sachet that came with her recent bottle of conditioner.

She might only be a thumbnail-sized picture in the bottom of a phone screen, but it didn't hurt to look as nice as she could in case Callum had Fergus sitting next to him—or, more disturbingly, took one of those screenshot things if that was possible.

Of course, there would be changes in them both. There couldn't not be after thirty-four years. But deep in her heart, the man in Ingrid's photo had stared straight at her with those beautiful, ocean-blue eyes as though beckoning her to him—and time had stood still.

36

Queensland, July 2024 – Ingrid

IMPATIENT FOR HER shift to end, Ingrid sent a quick text to her mother while she had a moment of patient-free time.

'Has she arrived yet?'

'No.'

'Good. Will be there in an hour or so. See you then.'

As she dropped her phone into her bag, a man stumbled through the emergency room entrance, his arm wrapped in a blood-soaked towel. Ingrid forced her mind away from Lucy's visit and hurried to greet him.

Almost two hours later, she arrived home, delighted to see a dusty SUV parked in their driveway.

Laughter greeted her from the lounge as she entered, and a relieved smile spread across her face. It had been a nerve-tingling visit to Dalgonally, but Ingrid was ecstatic with the reception Lucy had shown both her and her mother—and even more delighted to witness the two older women form a comfortable, understanding connection, as though they had been friends for years.

It seemed today was a continuation of that. Her heart skipped with joy. Since the search for Lucy began, Ingrid's emotions had surged and receded like the tide—or more appropriately, she likened it to riding a roller-coaster. From hope to disappointment, the one positive throughout had been Callum. With more messages and emails than she cared to count, plus their now almost daily calls depending on Ingrid's shifts, words had strengthened their friendship. Perhaps a little old-fashioned, but Ingrid considered it a wonderful way to get to know more about each other—especially as she didn't have much choice. Now she longed to see him again in person.

'We're in here, Ingrid,' Vonnie called.

Smiling, she hugged Lucy before pressing a kiss on her mother's face. 'Sorry I'm late. You never know what's going to happen in emergency, so my hours are often a little erratic.'

'That's fine, Ingrid. Don't apologise. I, too, was a nurse, although since my accident I haven't returned to full capacity.' Lucy shrugged. 'It seems memory loss and nursing don't really gel. Instead I've been working a couple of days a week at the aged care facility in town —still nursing in a way but without as many responsibilities.'

'That's amazing. Mum was also a nurse. Good to know we all speak the same language.' She laughed and plonked herself into a cream brocade armchair.

'It's a good career, despite its ups and downs,' Vonnie said. 'Midwifery was my forte, but I retired a couple of years ago, before Tony became unwell.'

They chatted about Tony's illness and shared experiences within the health system before Lucy asked, 'Have you always lived in Toowoomba?'

Vonnie shook her head. 'No, I was brought up on a farm near Clifton and while Ingrid and her brother, Rodney, have lived here most of their lives, Ingrid's not a total "townie". Being horse-mad as a child, she and I spent many hours on a friend's property a few kilometres away where we kept Ingrid's horse.'

'I joined pony club and was keen on dressage,' Ingrid added. 'But when I bought my unit, I didn't have the money or the time to continue competing. A friend loved Jonty, my horse, and when her parents offered me more money than I could afford to ignore, Becky took him over. The two of them have as good a relationship as the old boy and I did, and I'm grateful he has such a lovely home.'

They chatted for a further hour, Vonnie insisting Lucy stay with them overnight instead of in a motel. Satisfied with Lucy's acceptance, they sipped tea as they talked before moving on to a pre-dinner glass of wine and eventually, after dinner, shifted the conversation to the Isle of Skye.

'That roast lamb was delicious,' Lucy said. 'It reminds me of the dinners Peggy used to cook at the Ardvasar hotel.'

'Peggy?' Ingrid dropped her spoon in the now empty ramekin that, until a few seconds earlier, had contained her mother's delicious home-made crème caramel. She goggled at Lucy, her eyebrows raised. 'Peggy was there when you lived on Skye?'

'Yes. She was the manager, the chief chef—and one of the loveliest women I've ever met.' Blinking rapidly, she stared at Ingrid. 'You've got no idea how happy this makes me. Sharing memories of friends and experiences that I'd dismissed—even if unconsciously. All these years, I was oblivious to her existence and now ... well, I can't believe this is happening.'

Ingrid placed her hand over Lucy's. 'It's wonderful. I know you must be feeling rather discombobulated, but it'll pass,' she finished confidently, gathering the dessert plates as she stood. 'Give me a minute to load the dishwasher, then I'll grab my iPad and we'll call Callum.'

Lucy's eyes danced. Patting her mouth with her serviette, she said, 'Wonderful. I'll freshen my lipstick, so Callum doesn't think I'm too much of a country bumpkin.'

Vonnie chuckled. 'You look lovely. And I'm sure whatever transpires in this conversation, it will be good.'

LUCY FOCUSED ON TAKING DEEP, regular breaths as Ingrid explained Callum would be alone at his end and would take a screenshot of her to share with Fergus. Then, if she agreed, he and Ingrid would schedule another call for the following morning for a one-on-one conversation between Lucy and Fergus.

She waited as Ingrid tapped the iPad, her pulse racing so fast she thought she might faint.

The moment Callum's face filled the screen, Lucy was speechless. In every way except for his hair being slightly lighter in colour, she was looking at Fergus.

'Hello there,' he said, his smile widening as Ingrid leaned in, pressing her face next to Lucy's so he could see them both.

'Hi. As you can see, Lucy is here!'

'Fabulous. She exists!'

Finding her voice, Lucy returned the smile, adding, 'I most certainly do. And I am very grateful for your help in filling in a part of my life that I had accepted I'd lost.'

He grinned, his smile sending an electric shock through Lucy, his likeness to Fergus so strong it caught her breath.

'Actually, I feel guilty. Ingrid's done the leg work—and is still waiting to receive a result regarding a death certificate, not that it's important anymore—which is fabulous news. But the most amazing part of this ... reunion, is the coincidental meeting with Mandy at the hospital.'

Lucy laughed. 'I think Ingrid got the hint that Mandy and I didn't see a lot of one another—which I plan on rectifying now. She hardly ever comes inland —prefers to spend her holidays travelling elsewhere—so her visit to Toowoomba was quite out of character and I'd like to think that somewhere, the whole fortuitous meeting was meant to be.'

'I agree.' Callum paused, his face growing serious. 'Where do we go from here, Lucy? Are you up to having a chat with Fergus?'

Pink heat flushed her neck and she quivered. 'Yes please. I would like that more than anything.'

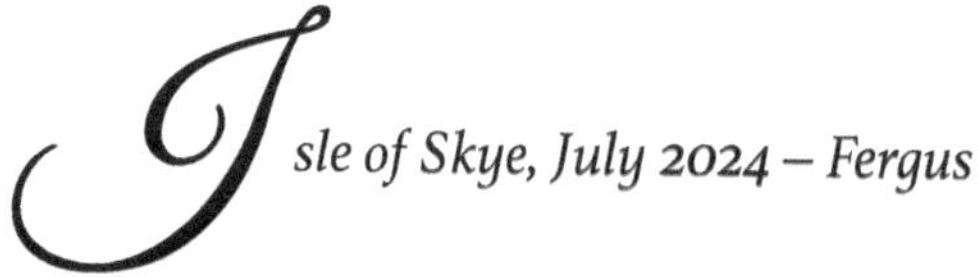

sle of Skye, July 2024 – Fergus

LIKE A FROG ON A HOT ROCK, Fergus couldn't keep still. He paced around his living room, opened and closed the front door several times, and eventually strode down the track to the farthest paddock on his farm, convincing himself the freshly cut grass needed checking before they could make silage.

His phone buzzed in his pocket, shocking him despite his anticipation of the call.

'Callum?'

'We've had a lovely talk. I've just sent you the screenshot I took of Lucy.'

Fergus fumbled with the phone, stabbing the

screen with his forefinger until the photo was revealed. He stopped dead in the middle of the track.

'So, what do you think?' Callum said. 'Can you see it alright?'

'Aye. I can.'

His face softened, his eyes prickling. Except for the slight alterations to her hair colour and style, she hadn't changed at all. It was Lucy—his Lucy. He staggered to the rock wall that edged the track and reached out to lower himself onto it. For thirty-four years he had dreamed of this moment. He'd battled depression and loss. But he'd never given up. She was alive. Did she want to talk to him?

'Ingrid thought you might like to talk to her yourself later. It's night-time in Australia now so they'll be off to bed shortly. Perhaps you could come here this evening after you've had a chance to think things over. I'll send Ingrid a message to check they're up—and then you and Lucy can talk tonight our time, morning in Australia.'

'Aye. Sounds good. I'll be there.'

They ended the call, but Fergus remained on the wall, staring at his phone and the face he loved. 'If equal affection cannot be, let the more loving be me!' he murmured.

Only perhaps, if you hadn't had your accident, hadn't lost those wonderful memories of our time together, our love would be equal.

In a daze, he plodded around the farm. The cut grass had wilted to the desired moisture level, but he barely registered his actions, instead relying on years of habit. After hooking the chopper to the rear of the tractor, he drove steadily around the field, stopping occasionally to re-check the cutters and moisture. As the machine chugged rhythmically, the extraordinary results of Ingrid's search for Lucy ticked through his head again and again. Callum had shared regular updates, but it had only been three days since his nephew had screeched to a halt outside Fergus's door and dashed into his kitchen with the news that Lucy had been found—and was alive and well. Even now, his chest tightened, his heart thumping as thoughts churned in his head. Would she want to reconnect with him? What had her life been like? Perhaps she wouldn't be interested in him after all this time?

After what felt more like a month than a day, he showered, shaved, and dressed in a clean shirt and jeans. Then he poured himself a whisky and sat on the chair outside his wee croft, watching the bees buzz around the flowers in the summer sunshine and listening to the hum of farm machinery and the bleat of sheep. The days were long although the solstice had passed and the midges would be arriving soon, as they did every evening at this time of year. As he considered the thought, he ran a hand over Pip's shoulders. 'Time to move, girl, before those wee devils get us. Callum will be waiting.'

His heart gave another hop of anxious anticipation. He swallowed the last mouthful of whisky.

FOR WHAT SEEMED like minutes but was much less, they stared at each other. Despite more than sixteen thousand kilometres separating them, the clarity was perfect. Fine streaks of grey added silvery lights to Lucy's rich brown hair, the tiny lines around her mouth stretching as she smiled. Her familiar deep green eyes reminded him of the rich grasses that covered the hills in summer, and he returned her smile.

'I'm sorry,' she said.

'So am I.' His voice was barely a whisper. 'Particularly for what you have been through. Callum told me.'

She nodded. 'You?'

'Not much changes here—except for growing older and hopefully wiser.'

Chuckling, she replied, 'It's better than the alternative.'

In an instant, Fergus wished he could bite back his words. Her parents had died, as had his. But, according to Callum, she had also lost her husband, father, and brother-in-law in a plane crash, and suffered a dreadful accident herself which had robbed her of more than he could imagine, including precious memories.

Seemingly oblivious to his regrets, Lucy continued, 'Are the blackberries fruiting? I remember us "brambling" as you called it. We don't have them where I live. Too hot and anyway, they're declared a pest so if anyone was to find some on their property, the plants would probably be poisoned. We can still buy them though. Farms farther south grow them commercially,' she rattled on breathlessly. Suddenly stopping, she raised a hand to her throat. 'Oh, I'm sorry for gabbling on. I … really don't know what to say.'

He chortled. 'You're doing alright—but I understand. I feel the same. Perhaps you could tell me about your farm? What do you do on it—and are you still nursing?'

Gradually, as each minute passed by, they both relaxed, answering each other's questions. Although remaining a little formal as though the call was their first meeting, Fergus's heartbeat slowed, the world behind him evaporated, and he found himself consumed with amazement that he was sitting in Callum's office, talking to the woman he had loved so deeply—and believed he still did.

He didn't want to end the call and yet he knew they had to. Each had a lot to think about—and if he had anything to do with it, it wouldn't be the last time they talked.

Drawing a deep breath, he smiled again. 'I guess we'd better get off this thing. Thank you for ringing me.'

'Will we talk again?' Her voice was so soft he could hardly hear the words. But he felt the emotion. The hope.

'We will. I'll get Callum to teach me how to do it.'

She laughed then. 'Yes, and I'll ask Ingrid to show me what to do at my end. Perhaps we could simply call each other on our cell phones—if you have one?'

'Oh yes. I have one—thanks to Callum. And yes, much as I've loved being able to talk face to face, sort of ... just hearing your voice would be better than nothing.'

They exchanged goodbyes at the exact moment Callum returned to the office. Nodding his consent, Callum removed the iPad from Fergus's grip and tapped the red icon.

Lucy disappeared as the screen went black, but Fergus wasn't concerned. They would talk again soon.

This was just the beginning.

38

———

 ueensland, July 2024 – Lucy

SHE STARED AT THE DEVICE, her mind spinning, before Ingrid waltzed into the room, a wide grin on her face.

'Well? How did it go?'

Lucy drew a breath and returned Ingrid's smile. 'It was perfect.'

'Great! So ... what's next?'

'We'll talk again. I'll return to the farm and think things over.' She hesitated for a moment. 'Would you show me how I phone Fergus—without the video thing? Our internet is rather unreliable at home so I'm not sure I would risk it and I'm definitely not driving over to Kylie and Matthew's, even if they have one of those satellite gadgets. Kylie is a wonderful friend, but I think I'd like to sort out my own thoughts before I share them.'

Ingrid nodded her understanding. 'Got it. Even though Adam and Meg know about Fergus now, you don't think they would tell them?'

Lucy shook her head firmly as Vonnie joined them. 'No. They respect my privacy and assured me they wouldn't breathe a word without my consent. I'm sure you've heard how stories travel fast in the country— and I don't doubt some will enjoy colouring the truth if it makes a good tale.'

'Looks like I missed the crucial bit?' Vonnie inclined her head, eyebrows raised in question. 'Did it go well?'

A sudden, spontaneous smile spread across Lucy's face. She stepped forward and hugged Vonnie. 'It did and I know it's early days, but ...' She ran her tongue over her lips before continuing, 'I think I need to go to Scotland.'

Ingrid whooped and both she and Vonnie hugged Lucy again as though they'd been friends forever.

'When?' Vonnie asked.

Lucy's shoulders drooped. 'Not immediately. I can't.'

Both women waited for her to continue, confusion on Ingrid's face and understanding on Vonnie's.

'These things take some planning—and I know you'll want to think on it,' Vonnie said.

'They do. I don't even have a passport!'

'I can help you there. The application doesn't take long to complete but you'll need passport photos and a couple of other things. I'll print the form off for you now and you can take it home, read it over, and then either come back here and we'll help you organise it or perhaps Adam or Meg will help you?' Ingrid waited for a tiny nod from Lucy before she dashed out of the room.

'Meg's wonderful with technology—because of her job.'

'What does she do?' Vonnie asked.

'Marketing. She manages the advertising, social media, and whatnot for a number of small businesses. It seems these days it's essential if you want to succeed. So she spends most of her days in the farm office over at the main homestead and now deals with the Dalgonally marketing as well.' Lucy's face twisted, her eyes sparkling as though about to burst with joy. 'She's been kept extra busy lately as she and Adam are getting married in September.'

Vonnie clapped her hands together. 'How lovely. Where will the wedding take place?'

'They've booked a place called Jimbour House. You've probably heard of it? It's a gorgeous sandstone home near Dalby.'

'Yes. I do know it although I've never visited. Do Meg's family live nearby?'

'No. They own a property near Longreach. According to Meg, her parents have offered to contribute to either a large, local wedding in the Longreach area or a smaller one in whichever venue Meg and Adam choose. With travel and accommodation to consider, thankfully it will be a relatively small affair—sixteen staying at the homestead and the other twenty will stay in town with a shuttle bus arranged for their travel.'

'Very organised.'

Lucy grinned and nodded. 'She is. And I'm delighted. If I had been fortunate enough to have had a daughter, I hope she would have been like Meg—or Ingrid.'

Ingrid reappeared at that moment and handed a sheaf of papers to Lucy. 'What's that about Ingrid? Am I coming with you to Scotland—I'll carry your bags?' she burbled hopefully.

'Now that's an idea,' Lucy said. 'I might have been full of confidence in 1990, but not so much now.' She lifted her gaze and met Vonnie's. 'What about you, Vonnie? Fancy a trip to the Isle of Skye?'

The initial shocked expression on Vonnie's face remained for less than five seconds. She smiled. 'Do you know what? I've always wanted to visit Scotland and never had the chance.'

'Well, Mum. Now it's here—and with it, your opportunity to meet Callum too.'

The room filled with a surge of sudden excitement as the suggestion took hold and they all began talking at once.

Lucy held up her hand. 'Please, just let me say this.' Both Vonnie and Ingrid stood in silence, their eyes fixed on Lucy's. 'It's quite strange that a week ago we didn't know each other. Now, here we are, planning a trip to the other side of the world and for me anyway, it feels like the most sensible decision I've made in thirty-four years.'

ON THE LONG DRIVE HOME, the events of the previous twenty-four hours circled her head a million times.

Fergus. Lined, grey-haired but still the man she had loved so deeply all that time ago. Ingrid, the vibrant young nurse who had randomly met a stranger in the Ardvasar Hotel, visited his croft, and heard his sad tale about the aerogrammes before deciding to take it upon herself to find Lucy.

She giggled out loud.

Perhaps Callum joining the scene may have created an ulterior motive there? Then there was Vonnie, a warm and caring woman who had recently lost her husband. Lucy knew what that felt like. With her old schoolfriends, Helen and Roslyn, living hundreds of kilometres away and them only connecting once or twice a year, Lucy had been drawn to Vonnie's warm, genuine soul. Perhaps it had been the sudden recollection of her memories that had woken her to the fact that friendships were important, even if you didn't reach out to one another regularly. While shared grief following the dreadful plane crash had brought her closer to Kylie, their friendship had remained family orientated—almost as though both deliberately kept their personal feelings and secrets to themselves in fear of the often-exaggerated bush telegraph. But on meeting Vonnie, an instant connection had greeted her —one that she hoped would flourish.

Queensland, September 2024 – Lucy

LUCY STOOD, waving to the final guests as they departed beautiful, peaceful Jimbour House.

As expected, Adam and Meg's wedding had been perfect. Everything including the faultless service, music, food, and weather had been exactly as they'd hoped. Spring flowers nodded gently in the breeze and a single, confident magpie ran across the lawn to within three metres of Lucy, lifted its head, and warbled.

Her eyes filled with unexpected tears at the perfection of the melody, beauty, and gratitude that the "event of the year" for her son and daughter-in-law was now over.

'Ready for home?'

Mandy's voice jolted her from her reverie, and she blinked away the tears as both her sister and Kylie joined her. 'Yes. Thank you. It's been a memorable weekend, hasn't it?'

'Absolutely magic. A great time of year for Adam and Meg to enjoy the Whitsundays too.' Kylie released a noisy sigh. 'Perhaps that's what Matthew and I need. It's nearly forty years since we had a proper holiday—without kids.'

Lucy shot her a rueful smile. 'I know. That's the hardest thing about farming, isn't it? Getting away for a break.'

Kylie shrugged. 'We're more fortunate than most. We both now have our boys to run the property and once you return from this Scottish trip, perhaps it will be our turn.'

Lucy's heart leapt, her veins fizzing with anticipation at her upcoming reunion with Fergus. In a little over two weeks, they would be together again on the other side of the world. In Ardvasar, possibly even in Fergus's croft, where they could pick up the pieces left there so long ago.

An urgency heightened her colour—and her enthusiasm. 'I'm ready for home. Give me a few minutes to collect my things.'

'I'll head off too,' Mandy said. 'Got lots to do—as usual.' She opened her arms and enveloped Lucy in a surprisingly long hug. 'You take care now and have a good time. Message me whenever you can—and don't forget to share photos now that I've shown you how to do it.' She paused for a beat. 'What a bummer you didn't own a camera back in 1990. That may have changed your life completely.'

Lucy grimaced. 'Let's not go there—and yes, ma'am, I will keep in contact.' She hugged her back.

Mandy looked her sister up and down. 'By the way, you look lovely today, Lucy. That turquoise colour suits you—and you're lucky your hair is still so thick and you haven't had to battle the weight issue I have.'

Lucy grinned. Her sister's compliment was both rare and inspiring. Some days she felt every minute of her fifty-eight years. But today she had felt young again, probably buoyed by the knowledge of what lay ahead, she mused.

Mandy kissed Kylie and, with a brief hand-wave, marched off toward her car, while Lucy watched her go.

Since her letter-tidying revelation, Mandy seemed to have unexpectedly softened toward her. Lucy wasn't sure if it was because of guilt, or something else. Perhaps it was simply because she'd realised that, with the exception of Adam, the only family members left were the two of them—sisters who, for much of their lives, had never been friends. A warm glow grew inside her. Blood ties didn't always bond siblings, but joyful satisfaction filled her soul knowing that their sisterly relationship was stronger now than it had ever been—and was growing ever more solid.

As she wheeled her bag into the carpark minutes later, she straightened her back, allowing the smile to creep across her face.

It had been a hectic two months. With fortnightly visits to Vonnie and Ingrid's, they had completed all the arrangements. Her passport had arrived, and flights, a hire car, and accommodation were booked. Ingrid had even remembered the ferry crossing and had made a reservation for that. They had shopped together for suitable clothing, power adaptors, light-weight toiletries, and RFID-protected wallets.

At last, everything was done.

Now that the wedding, calving, and the daily harvesting of spring foliage were behind her, she would spend the two weeks of Adam and Meg's absence giving the homestead a thorough clean.

Then she would prepare for the moment she had been waiting for—returning to the Isle of Skye.

EVERY DAY, she and Fergus spoke via either a video or phone call, and every day, more memories returned to each of them as they relived the months prior to receiving Mandy's panicked, demanding request for Lucy to return to Australia.

Adeptly adjusting to using video calls, courtesy of both Callum and Ingrid's instructions, Lucy stared at Fergus, consuming the smile lines etched around his mouth, the ocean-blue of his eyes, and she longed to reach out and touch his face.

'Not long now,' he said.

It was the evening of Adam and Meg's return to Dalgonally. Lucy would drive to Toowoomba and stay overnight with Vonnie and Ingrid before continuing the journey with them to Brisbane the following day for the long, anticipated flight.

Unable to keep the smile from her face, she nodded. 'Two more days, give or take a few hours.'

'I wish you'd let me pick you up from Glasgow airport.'

'I know.' There was nothing she wanted more than to be with Fergus as soon as possible, but common sense prevailed. 'We'll be tired and jet-lagged, so staying the first night at Arrochar will allow us to catch up on sleep before we continue to Mallaig the next morning. Also, Vonnie and Ingrid will need the rental car for independence, so it makes sense for us to drive.'

'I've got a few things planned for us,' he said.

'Great—I think?'

He guffawed. 'Aye. You're thinking of the calf sales I mentioned yesterday?'

'Yep.'

'Well. Maybe that will fit somewhere into the three weeks you'll be here, but I was thinking about you and me escaping for a few days.'

'Where to?'

'A friend of mine has offered to take us over to the Isle of Rum in his boat. He's got a wee guesthouse there.'

Heat surged through Lucy's body. Fergus's plans were beginning to sound astonishingly intimate. Was that what she wanted this soon?

'Oh,' she squeaked.

'Dinna worry. We may not get there if the weather turns.' He paused, his face softening. 'Remember I was going to take you there to see Kinloch Castle in 1990? Since then, tourism has moved on but it's late in the season and not so busy at the moment.'

She chided herself for being silly. They were grown adults and she was perfectly able to control both her emotions and her actions. A private getaway would be a wonderful opportunity to be themselves. To not be distracted by chores, animals, or family. To talk, laugh, and share good times and bad. They may discover that anything more than platonic friendship was out of reach—and that, she convinced herself, would be fine.

SHE LAY STARING through the cabin window late that night. The curtains were open—as they had been when her father lived there and now, sharing his dislike of being shut in, they were again pulled to the side, allowing silvery light from the full moon to fill the room.

I'm fifty-eight. Am I doing the right thing? Or am I fooling myself.

Self-recriminations swirled inside her head. Her life was different now. She belonged here in western Queensland where she'd been born, grown up, and lived for the majority of her life. She adored farm life. Although the summer heat was becoming less tolerable as every year moved on.

Outside, a boobook owl hooted seconds before the whoosh of wings scooted past the open window. The scent of freshly cut lucerne drifted in. She closed her eyes, willing sleep to come.

This time tomorrow, I'll be at the airport—and after that, I'll be in Scotland.

Her insides tumbled as raw panic flittered through her. Rolling onto her side, she curled into a ball and breathed deeply. Her body became heavy as the memory of salt air wafted through her mind, accompanied by the image of purple, heather-clad hills in the distance. She drifted into a deep, trouble-free sleep.

ctober 2024

'YOU'LL NEVER GUESS who phoned me this morning,' Ingrid announced with wide eyes.

'Who?' Lucy barely looked up as she dragged her suitcase from the rear of her Prado. The arrangement was for Lucy to leave her vehicle in Toowoomba and Ingrid to drive the three of them to Rodney and Laura's home. Rodney would then deliver them to the airport, leaving Ingrid's little car safely tucked up in their garage for the duration of the holiday.

'Dan. From the Roma post office.'

Lucy dropped the bag on the path and stared at Ingrid with raised eyebrows.

'You wouldn't believe it—he rang to tell me he'd attended a local football club party recently and heard someone mention Binnalong. He questioned them and discovered it was an elderly local who used to deliver the mail out that way in the nineties. He said it had been joined to the Dalgonally Enterprise after "the wife died and the daughter had an accident". This fellow—Dan—said he didn't know the name of the owners but thought he'd ring me and let me know about the amalgamation of the two properties. Thought it might help.'

'That's amazing. What did you tell him?'

'I think he was a bit disappointed his information wasn't the magical discovery he'd thought it was—but said he was pleased to hear we'd found you anyway.'

'That was very kind of him, dear,' Vonnie said as she added her bag to the pile in front of the garage. 'Now come on. I know it's still six hours before our flight leaves, but we've got to be there three hours beforehand and you never know what the highway will be like.'

For the next fifteen minutes, they organised luggage, locked Lucy's car away, cast a final glance around the house ensuring nothing had been forgotten, and piled into the vehicle.

Lucy's stomach spun cartwheels as she looked through the back window and watched Toowoomba slide away into the distance.

I can't believe it. We're finally on our way to Scotland!

THE FLIGHT WAS long and arduous. Lucy couldn't remember it being so tiring years earlier. *Probably because I was young then.* Her head and body felt heavy and her neck ached from trying to sleep, despite using the neck pillow Ingrid insisted they all take.

She and Vonnie had sat beside the luggage at Glasgow airport while Ingrid sorted out the hire car.

Finally, as the afternoon was drawing in and a deep purple glow appeared on the horizon, the three women, their little blue hatchback piled high with luggage, wended their way onto the highway for the forty-five-minute drive to the Arrochar guesthouse.

THE FOLLOWING MORNING, Lucy rose and padded barefoot to the window. Despite grey skies, her now-rested body fizzed with excitement as she gazed at the vista. The loch, surrounded by hills covered in foliage and grass of every hue, glinted in the morning light.

She glanced at her watch. Too early for the scheduled eight o'clock breakfast, she took the three steps required to reach the tiny cabinet in the corner of the room and switched on the electric jug. Although the weather looked blustery outside, she acknowledged it was October and winter wasn't far away. With the curtains pushed wide open and her hands wrapped around the mug of tea, she slid back into bed and sipped her drink, reluctant to drag her eyes away from the peaceful outside scene.

A gentle knock sounded on her door. 'Are you awake, Lucy?'

'Yes, Ingrid. Hang on.'

After replacing the mug on the bedside table, she opened the door to greet Ingrid. Fully dressed in jeans and a warm, maroon-coloured jumper, Ingrid's face glowed, her smile wide and her eyes sparkling.

'Did you sleep okay?' she asked.

'Yes,' Lucy said. 'Like a log. I don't even remember getting under the doona.'

'Me too. I'm glad we stayed here though. Much better than arriving on Skye tired and dishevelled— even if we'd got the last ferry of the day.'

'I agree.' Lucy crossed her hands over her breast-bone. 'I'm so excited though. I just want to get on that road and get to Skye now.'

'Same. Mum's in the shower but won't be long. Why don't you get organised, and we'll pack the car before we eat breakfast.'

'Perfect.' Lucy placed a hand on Ingrid's arm, turned her around, and gently pushed her toward the door. 'Off you go. I'll see you downstairs in thirty minutes.'

MEMORIES FLOODED BACK in waves as they crossed the sound, the chug of the boats' engines beating in time with her own heart. Vague images of a rain-shrouded Armadale crossed Lucy's mind—of the aching sense of loss and heartbreaking worry about her mother that had weighed heavily on her thirty-four years earlier.

She closed her eyes for a second, breathing in the damp, salty air and counting down the minutes as the gap closed between the ferry and the shore.

An arm tucked into hers and she turned to smile at Ingrid. Placing her hand on Ingrid's, she faced the pretty young woman's excited grin.

'I can't thank you enough for this. If it hadn't been for your determination—and possibly for falling in love with a Scotsman ...' Lucy held up her hand, stalling the obvious retort Ingrid was about to share, 'I wouldn't be here now.'

Ingrid tilted her head to one side. 'I'm not so sure about that. Mandy may have remembered those letters one day—or your amnesia may have healed all by itself and everything could have come back to you?'

Sitting opposite, Vonnie exchanged a smile with both Ingrid and Lucy. 'Knowing my daughter as I do, I suspect—being a passionate romance reader and having an inquisitive nature—Ingrid would have followed up the mystery of those letters—even without Fergus's permission.'

They laughed as the loudspeaker announced their impending arrival at the Armadale pier.

Lucy's stomach began somersaulting again as she stood and peered through the window. Fergus had said he would be waiting.

At first, she thought her eyesight might be failing. Not one but two tall, broad-shouldered men stood side-by-side on the edge of the carpark. As the ferry docked, the clouds parted and the sun shone down, illuminating the waiting crowd.

Lucy's breath caught, jamming in her throat.

Skye. I'm here. I've returned.

ike a lost puppy, Lucy followed Ingrid and Vonnie back to their car and minutes later they drove onto the pier, parking beside a dark green Land Rover.

Ingrid launched herself out of the driver's seat and ran toward Callum. They hugged, kissed, and then he lifted her off the ground and spun in a circle.

Left standing on his own, Fergus smiled, stepped forward, and reached for Lucy's hands. Gripped in their warmth, Lucy's eyes met his and the world stood still.

'Welcome back.'

'Thank you.'

Their voices were soft, filled with disbelief.

'This is my mother, Vonnie,' Ingrid announced.

'And this is Callum.' She grasped her mother's hand with a beaming smile.

While Vonnie exchanged pleasantries with Callum, Lucy and Fergus remained glued to the spot. Unable to think about anyone or anything except the man standing in front of her, Lucy simply smiled.

Fergus wore a pale-coloured striped shirt, a faded, well-worn tie of sapphire blue, and a thick tweed jacket bearing the faint scents of sheep and Ralph Lauren Polo aftershave. She felt a sudden urge to bury her face into his chest and close her eyes but instead, she pinned her gaze on his.

'It's good to see you.' His voice was slightly clearer than on their calls but with a huskiness she put down to the same emotional energy her own emitted.

'Peggy's waiting for us at the pub,' Callum said, seemingly reluctant to release Ingrid's hand. 'Why don't you go with Fergus, Lucy, and I'll jump in this wee rental car with Ingrid and Vonnie?'

Fergus opened the Land Rover door, and she slid onto the seat, inhaling the smells of sheep and dog.

His hand slid over to hers again, clasping it firmly in his as though afraid he would lose her. 'Thank you for coming back. I can't believe this is happening, even though I've longed for it since the day you left.'

She nodded slowly. 'I know. It's surreal to me too—I hope it's not too late?'

'No. It's never too late.'

The years vanished in an instant. Despite more tourists flanking the road and the weather seeming cooler than on her previous visit, she felt like she had then—young, vibrant, and with a whole new life ahead of her.

INSIDE THE ARDVASAR HOTEL, Peggy greeted them with warm hugs before showing the women to their rooms and, minutes later, ushering everyone into the dining room.

It was full of people—some familiar faces for Ingrid, including Anna who enveloped her in a bear hug as though they were long-lost friends.

Callum's parents were there—Neil and Shauna—who Ingrid had not met but was delighted with the warm welcome they gave her. Another woman was introduced as Fiona, the travel agent who, thirty-four years earlier, had ensured Lucy was on the first available plane home to Australia. There were a few others Ingrid vaguely recognised, but her attention wasn't on any of them. She had eyes only for Callum.

An arm encircled her shoulders, drawing her to him. She leaned against him and released a long sigh.

By the strength of his embrace, it seemed he felt the same.

Drinks were dispensed and the noise increased in

the room before the waft of roast meat, vegetables, and various other fragrances drifted around them.

Ingrid was starving, diving into the food with gusto. She glanced across the table to where Lucy and Fergus sat together, her mother on the other side of Fergus and Neil and Shauna at either ends of the table. Grinning to herself, her thoughts touched on the table arrangement. Fergus was clearly not going to leave Lucy's side, regardless of the fact that, according to Callum, he always sat at the head of the table.

Eventually, with a spread of desserts finishing off the meal and coffee following, the MacRaes, Lucy, Ingrid, and Vonnie thanked Peggy and moved to the hotel lounge.

'I thought you might like to go for a walk,' Fergus said. 'The sun's shining and it's a shame to miss it.'

Everyone tittered. Here on Skye, sunshine was less common than rain and not to be missed.

'We could have a walk around the farm perhaps. Or the village—and maybe up to the common?' Fergus suggested tentatively.

'That sounds like a great idea,' Ingrid said. She glanced at her mother. 'You up for it, Mum?'

'Of course. That would be lovely. A chance to stretch our legs after all that time sitting on the plane. Although, much as I'm looking forward to seeing your wee croft Fergus, I think it would be nicer if you and Lucy had some time together before we visit.'

LUCY'S CHEST TIGHTENED. She could have hugged Vonnie. Unable to explain why, she wanted her return to the croft to be with Fergus—and no one else. She shot Vonnie a relieved smile of gratitude and, unless her eyesight was playing up, Vonnie gave her the tiniest wink in return.

The moment she stepped through the front porch into the kitchen, she was home. Not the airy, wood-floored homestead of Binnalong, but the cosy, solid walls that wrapped her in their arms, the scent of peat burning in the grate, and the fragrance of lemon and beeswax furniture polish filling her senses.

'Remember when we came here just before the ceilidh?' Fergus asked. 'You were worried Grandma would want to move back in. We discussed what changes we would make.'

She nodded. 'Yes. I remember,' she whispered. 'You've made those changes—and I love them.'

Running her hand over the wooden bench, she smiled. It was perfect. Its rich surface, protective, lacquered coating smooth and waterproof, felt warm under her touch. Soft green cupboards filled the space below with another row of smaller cabinets fixed to the wall above the electric stove, a sparkling exhaust fan unobtrusively fitted to the underside.

Although not a modern kitchen in the sense of

appliances, the view through the window above the sink unit was one Lucy would never tire of. The vista—wide, filled with sheep-filled fields, houses dotted randomly down lanes leading to the village, and beyond them, the ever-changing grey-blue of the sea.

'Have a look at the rest of the house while I make tea,' Fergus said.

Wordlessly, she trailed through the cottage, awestruck by the brand-new bathroom, the tidy, book-lined office, and the spare bedroom which, the last time she had visited, had contained two narrow beds where Neil and Fergus had spent childhood nights. Now the walls were freshly wallpapered in a soft, autumn pattern. A cream-coloured quilt covered the double bed, a thick rug on the floor.

Returning to the living room, she met Fergus's nervous nod.

'Check out the main bedroom.'

She pushed the door open and stepped inside. It was exactly as she remembered it when Fergus and Neil's grandmother had left. Now a newer, colourful homemade quilt covered the bed and thick, warm carpet was soft under her feet. Dragging her gaze to the window, her breath stalled. Facing away from the sea, coloured hills led to rugged, rocky outcrops, and beyond them, the deeply bruised tones of the early winter sky.

'That quilt was the last thing Mum made before

she died. Grandma taught her and Shauna found it in the chest she'd kept her sewing in. When you said you were coming over, she gave it to me. Said she thought you'd like it.' He spoke softly, his voice filled with hope and pride.

'It's beautiful, Fergus. The whole house is beautiful. You've done a fabulous job of updating—and it looks to be very recent?'

He chuckled. 'It was. After Ingrid's visit earlier in the year, I went through a turbulent couple of months —hoping like mad that she'd find you but never knowing when or what she'd discover. Would you be happily married? Disinterested in reconnecting with me? Anyway, it was something that I've wanted to do for decades. A bit of a disgrace really, I suppose, leaving it as it was. So, while I waited to hear the best news of my life, I kept busy making it the nicest home I could.'

She smiled up at him and tucked her arm into his. 'I'm impressed.'

He released an audible whoosh of breath and pulled out a kitchen chair. 'Sit down and have your tea. Then I'll run you back to the hotel and perhaps we can make plans for our time together?'

Her chest tightened with hope. Three whole weeks. She and Fergus had been handed a second chance and whatever they did and wherever they visited, every-thing would be perfect.

42

The first ten days of their holiday passed in a rush. As a group, Fergus and Callum put all but the essential farm chores to one side as they escorted the three women to favourite haunts, breathtakingly scenic walks, and historical sites. As every day dawned cool but fine, the opportunities to remain outdoors were too good to miss so they packed the vehicles with Peggy's picnic baskets and headed to a different part of the Isle, often returning well after dark.

Evenings were mostly spent either at the hotel or at Neil and Shauna's home where, after their meal, Callum and Ingrid escaped to Callum's annexe, leaving the others to socialise.

While grateful for the MacRae family's hospitality, Lucy was a little surprised to acknowledge a sense of panic growing inside her. Conversations with Fergus had been fewer than when they were phoning each other regularly. She didn't like abandoning Vonnie— after all, they had agreed to travel together. However, their time on Skye was passing quickly and although she was enjoying every moment, thoughts of the future clutched at her. Had she been kidding herself that friendship was enough for her and Fergus?

Almost at the end of the second week, the weather changed and they woke to pouring rain and gale-force winds.

Fergus arrived at the hotel midmorning, alone, and despite shedding his coat and hat in the boot room, water dripped off his hair onto his collar as Lucy greeted him.

'It's wild out there,' he said as they walked into the lounge. 'Would you like to spend the day at the croft with me?'

Lucy glanced across the room to where Vonnie was sitting in the corner reading a book. Ingrid had left in the rental car an hour earlier, announcing that she was helping Callum "in his office". Lucy wasn't sure what that entailed and hadn't asked. She was just pleased that the reunion between the two of them had been so enthusiastic and appeared to be strengthening as each day went by.

As though sensing Lucy's hesitation, Vonnie looked up from her book and smiled. 'Please accept my apologies if you're planning another outing today. I'm rather weary and would like to have a quiet day to myself.'

Gratitude surged through Lucy. Vonnie was the most intuitive person she'd ever met—and she loved her for her understanding.

SHE STOOD by the fire in the croft, warming her hands while Fergus poured the tea, longing to forget about sipping on hot drinks and instead press herself against his chest, encircled in his arms. It had been so long since she'd experienced any form of desire for a man. She couldn't recall her relationship with Robert being particularly physical, but she guessed it must have been. They were young and back then, she had believed she loved him.

But the feeling that burned through her body bore no resemblance to those days—or to Robert. This was something visceral, raw, and so deep she couldn't describe it. She only knew that she wanted the last thirty-four years to fade away, leaving the two of them as they were in 1990.

Fergus looked up at her, his irises darkening as they met hers. As though reading her mind, he ignored the tea, moved toward her, and gathered her in his arms.

They remained motionless for a few seconds

before she lifted her face to his. The years fell away and they were one again. She closed her eyes as he kissed her, softly at first then deepening, urgently.

Drawing a breath, their gazes met and slowly, silently, they walked across the room, entered the bedroom, and closed the door behind them.

IN CALLUM'S ANNEXE, Ingrid lay beside him, her head resting on his shoulder and his arms around her, the depth of her love for him strong and encompassing.

'So much for finishing that website you're supposed to be building,' she laughed.

Callum squeezed her. 'We've got to make the most of every day—and today the weather gods are listening.'

'Are you saying you haven't enjoyed traipsing all over Skye?'

'Oh, aye. That's been grand—but this is better.'

He kissed her again as though to demonstrate the strength of his words and another hour passed.

Eventually, they returned to the kitchen, both declaring they were ravenous. As they threw together a pile of toast and an enormous omelette, their conversation grew serious.

'I don't want you to leave,' Callum said, his earnest voice deep with emotion.

'Neither do I.' She chewed her lip. 'I've been thinking.'

'Oh, aye,' he said with a grin.

She gave him a shove and chuckled. 'I mean it. I'm eligible for a British passport as my grandparents were born here. That means I could apply for whatever visas are appropriate and work in Scotland.'

His eyes widened as he stared into hers. A flash of something she couldn't recognise passed over his face. Shock?

Her heart thumped as a sudden chill ran down her spine. Had she presumed too much? Overestimated his feelings? Was it too early? She'd believed searching for Lucy and visiting Skye had strengthened their relationship. But perhaps she'd got it wrong.

A wide beam spread across his face, and she almost fainted with relief.

'That would be grand. Perhaps you could work at the Broadford Hospital? We could work it out. It's not too far to travel from here.'

She returned his grin, threw her arms around his neck, and pressed her lips against his.

'Getting the relevant paperwork sorted and staying here with me sounds like a pretty good plan,' he said.

'I'll have to go home first—we've got tickets for next week, remember, and I can get the ball rolling then.' She inclined her head. 'You mentioned you'd like to visit Australia?'

'I would. I'd go to Antarctica or Timbuktu if you asked me to—as long as we can be together.'

'Really?' Her body lightened, as though floating through space while she felt her head would explode with joy.

'Absolutely. We'll visit the hospital tomorrow and while that's being sorted out, we'll book my flights. I'm joining you in Australia for Christmas.'

43

———

On the final Tuesday of their holiday, the skies once again cleared and the five of them sat in the hotel lounge discussing their plans.

'Peggy has four days off and has invited me to join her on a visit to the Isle of Lewis,' Vonnie announced. 'We'll stay with her sister and drive around both Harris and Lewis like tourists.' She laughed. 'Peggy said it's years since she did anything spontaneous. I think she's looking forward to it as much as I am.'

Ingrid beamed. 'That's wonderful, Mum. You both seem to get along well and I'm sure Peggy would love your company.'

'What about you, Ingrid?' Lucy asked.

Ingrid and Callum exchanged a look, grins on their faces.

'We're off to Broadford tomorrow. Employment

enquiries to make and flights to book. Callum is coming to Australia for Christmas.'

Callum grasped Ingrid's hand as everyone voiced their delight.

'What about you, Lucy?' Ingrid murmured, her eyes bright and full of hope.

Lucy met Fergus's gaze and gave a tiny nod. 'We're not sure yet. I have a lot to think about with the farm and I'm not sure that Fergus would enjoy a Queensland summer.'

Fergus interjected. 'But whatever we decide, we'll let you all know after our visit to Rum.'

'Well. That's settled then,' Vonnie said. 'I'm going upstairs to sort out my clothes and repack for Lewis. Then I'm going to visit the museum again. Such a lot of wonderful history. I couldn't take it all in the first time.'

'I'd better get away home, Lucy,' Fergus said. 'The sheep need attention and I'll discuss the chores with Neil. He'll care for Pip while we're away and keep an eye on things at the croft.'

'I'll come with you,' she said, rising to her feet.

A flurry of action followed as, one by one, they abandoned the lounge.

FOR THE NEXT FOUR DAYS, Lucy marvelled at their good luck. Although cold, the weather remained fine, the gentle breezes just enough to remind them of the impending winter as white-capped waves rolled onto the shore.

The tiny guesthouse on the Isle of Rum was perfect, while the absence of tourists provided them with the privacy they craved. After visiting Kinloch Castle, they spent their days walking along the beaches, discussing events from their missed years, laughing, and most of all, sharing their love.

On their final day, an hour before Ken, Fergus's friend, would arrive to collect them in his boat, Fergus drew Lucy onto one of the chairs they'd moved to the small front veranda. Then he fished in his pocket and reached for her hand.

'I planned this moment over thirty-four years ago, and now it's finally here.' He chuckled. 'It's been a long wait, and this has been in the drawer all that time.'

Lucy looked down as he slid the dainty ring on her finger. Surrounded with tiny diamonds and sapphires, the band of gold was elegant, beautiful, and utterly unexpected.

She gasped. 'Really?'

'Yes, really. I don't know anyone who has waited as long as we have to be together, and I promise I will be with you every moment possible until we die.'

'Oh, Fergus.' Lucy's face crumpled as she held him to her, tears trickling down her face. 'It's the most beautiful ring I've ever seen—and I promise you ...

once we've crossed all the legal hurdles and you've visited Australia to see my farm and understand me better, I will return here and we'll never be apart again.'

'CAN YOU BELIEVE IT?' Ingrid gabbled excitedly, smiling across the table as they shared a magnificent farewell dinner the day before they were due to fly to Australia. 'One of the nurses is retiring in February. I've submitted my application and the Hospital Manager seemed quite confident that there would be plenty of work for me.'

'That's lovely,' Vonnie said. 'I suppose that will mean I'll need to plan annual Scottish holidays—perhaps I'll choose a different season each year?' she finished thoughtfully, and everyone laughed.

'What did you think of Lewis—and Harris?' Callum leaned forward, his gaze meeting Vonnie's.

'Glorious. Absolutely beautiful.' She paused, narrowing her eyes. 'I was lucky we had such lovely weather. I imagine it could have been quite different if it had teamed rain the whole time. Not that harsh weather would have prevented me from finding new friends. Nancy, Peggy's sister, was a wonderful host and we did enjoy our time together. We shopped, dined out, visited the historical black houses and other sites—and did a lot of talking while playing cards.'

Lucy said nothing. With her hand resting in Fergus's massive palm, her whole being sang with silent joy. Although saying goodbye the following morning would be difficult, it wouldn't come close to their farewell in 1990. This time she had Christmas to look forward to and in the weeks leading up to it, there would be a lot to discuss with Adam and Meg.

This time she and Fergus would alter the mantra he had dwelt on since her last departure, except that it would now be with some improvements:

"Our equal affection will always be, me for you and you for me."

EPILOGUE

emperatures soared, peaking at thirty-five degrees by midday on the Binnalong veranda. Huffing with relief, Lucy glanced around the room with a satisfied smile.

The new air-conditioning unit blew cold air over them with almost complete silence, unlike the previously well-used and struggling version that had been the first item to be replaced on her return to Australia. Couches and armchairs had been pushed against the walls and into corners, allowing for cloth-covered camp tables to fill the centre of the room.

'Where do you want this, Mum?' Adam staggered in carrying a large esky filled with ice.

'Over there, please.' She pointed to the corner where a card table laden with glasses and a full bowl of fruit punch sat. 'Pop it underneath the table.'

The sound of an approaching vehicle drew Lucy to the kitchen window.

'They're here!' she called, reaching to touch the large hand that rested gently on her shoulder. Grasping it, she swung around and planted a quick kiss on the rugged, familiar face. 'Come on. I can't wait to hear how Ingrid and Callum's trip to the Whitsundays went.'

'Hello!' Ingrid called. Struggling with parcels, she lifted the gate latch with her elbow and leaned forward to kiss Lucy on the cheek.

Vonnie and Callum followed, Vonnie carefully balancing a large container in both hands and Callum lugging overnight bags.

'Anyone would think we've come for a week,' he retorted.

'Well. You never know. You're welcome to stay as long as you like,' Lucy said, her smile widening.

Clattering through the kitchen and into the lounge, their loads were deposited and hugs were shared.

'The house looks lovely! So festive.' Vonnie breathed happiness as she gazed around the room. Tiny fairy lights and tinsel crisscrossed the ceiling and in front of the fireplace, a modest and stylishly decorated Christmas tree took pride of place.

Lucy laughed. 'We don't have much space to overdo things in this house, but it's always fun to make it as pretty as we can.' She flicked a hand toward Meg.

'Thankfully Meg is creative—and it's been wonderful having Fergus here to reach all those places I couldn't.'

Vonnie arranged the gifts around the pile already surrounding the tree, while Christmas carols poured from the speaker on the mantlepiece and the chatter rose.

'Are we all here now?' Ingrid asked as she counted them aloud and waited for Lucy's nod.

'Yes,' Mandy said as she spooned punch into eight glasses and handed them out. 'A refreshing drink to start—and then you can crack open the bubbly, Adam.' She nodded toward her nephew with a soft smile.

'Matthew and Kylie will pop over tomorrow for lunch. As usual, they've got hoards at their place today but by then they'll be back to manageable numbers,' Lucy added.

'Great. It will be nice to meet them all,' Ingrid said. 'And it's especially good that Fergus is here—even if it took a bit of coaxing to get him on that plane.'

Everyone chuckled. Fergus's fear of flying had been unknown weeks earlier. But, after more than one sleepless night filled with worry, he had shared his secret with both Lucy and Callum—and eventually succumbed to their encouragement after Callum promised he would be with him for every step of the way.

'You're looking a bit pale, Uncle.' Callum pushed

his sleeves up, exposing his bronzed skin. 'Look at this. Who knew a Scot could get such a good tan?'

'God, man. I've spent all my time here hiding from the sun. It's like a blowtorch!' Fergus snorted. 'Mind you, that tractor's got a good air-con system so I've quite enjoyed helping harvest the last of the barley.'

'Everyone ready for a drink?' Adam called.

It was midafternoon by the time Christmas dinner had been consumed and the cleaning up completed. For Fergus and Callum's benefit, Lucy had baked a lamb roast and vegetables but also incorporated the flavours of Queensland in the feast—prawns, mangoes, and Vonnie's homemade pavlova loaded with berries, shaved chocolate, and with passionfruit dripping down the sides.

Armed with more drinks, they flopped into chairs and on the lounge floor as Adam began handing out gifts.

Colourful wrapping paper was cast aside as Fergus and Callum immediately plonked their new Akubras on their heads, Vonnie exuded delight at her brightly coloured silk scarf, and Meg and Ingrid oohed and ahh'd at their pretty earrings.

While everyone was exchanging compliments and

thanks, Lucy quietly rose and fetched an envelope from behind the clock.

Handing it to Ingrid, she smiled softly. 'It seems good things are kept behind clocks. This one is for you, from me.'

Narrowing her eyes in question, Ingrid opened the envelope. A flight voucher fluttered into her lap. Picking it up, she stared at it for a moment before her wide eyes met Lucy's.

'Oh, Lucy. This is so generous of you.' Her lip quivered as she slid the voucher back into the envelope. 'There's something else here.' Removing the folded piece of pale blue paper, a quizzical frown formed on her face.

'What is it, love?' Vonnie asked.

Ingrid looked up at Lucy again. 'It's a letter from Lucy.'

'Read it out,' Mandy said firmly.

Ingrid's lip quivered again, and she nodded.

Dear Ingrid,

Six months ago, I could never have dreamed that we would all be sitting here together, not only celebrating Christmas but also revelling in the amazing events we've experienced.

None of us know what tomorrow will bring—and I've certainly learned that lesson more than once—so this is a special thank you for coming into our lives, bringing hope and second chances.

Thanks to your enquiring mind, kind heart, and dogged determination, you have provided us with more joy than we could ever have imagined.

This is just the beginning of a long life filled with love, family, and gratitude. I am delighted that we will be both friends and neighbours on the Isle of Skye.

Thanks to you—and those blue letters—our hearts are free once more.

With all our love,

Lucy and Fergus

Ingrid choked back a sob and hugged Lucy first, and then Fergus.

'You know me now. I love a good romance story. And ...' she smiled at Callum then faced Lucy and Fergus again, 'apart from ours, yours is the best yet.'

THE END

ACKNOWLEDGMENTS

Letters in Blue was inspired by a dream I had one night—a memory of something that happened when I lived on the Isle of Skye decades ago. An unanswered question concerning a stoic, friendly Scottish farmer who had lost touch with an old friend. In the dead of night, his words flashed through my mind and in that moment, I knew I had to write a story, even if fictitious.

I have so many people to thank for helping me along this journey, especially my Scottish friends: Millie and Janette who answered my many simple and complicated questions. Thank you ladies, for your wealth of knowledge and patience. Any mistakes made regarding farming and life on the Isle of Skye are entirely my own.

Huge thanks to my support crew and early readers, Dianne, Jennifer, Kathie, Patricia, Julia, Deb and Carly. Your enthusiasm for this story gave me the boost I needed and I can't thank you enough. Thanks also to my special author group friends, Phillipa, Michelle and Susan, who are my constant sounding board and mentors in every situation, book-related or not!

Thank you Anna and Lauren (CreatingINK) for your professional editing and support. A special thanks to Patti Roberts (Paradox Book Covers) for designing the beautiful cover—I love it and it says it all.

As always, loving thanks go to my husband, Roger, for his willingness to listen to me read my books, for his constant patience when I'm too busy at my desk to help him outside, and for his ongoing encouragement.

And last, but by no means least, thank you readers. Without you, there would be no reason to write.

ALSO BY HEATHER REYBURN

Tullagulla Series

The Cedar Tree

The English Oak

The Pepperina Grove

A Tullagulla Christmas

Fantail Ridge Series

Peninsula Promises

The Lupin Fields

The Scent of Promise

Featherwood Falls Series

A Stranger in Featherwood Falls

Secrets in Featherwood Falls

Sparks Fly in Featherwood Falls

Clouds over Featherwood Falls

Coming Home to Featherwood Falls

A Festive Featherwood Falls

AFTERWORD

If you enjoyed this book, I would love you to leave a review on your preferred site. Reviews encourage authors to continue writing and also help other readers to find my books.

Thank you for reading "Letters in Blue".

ABOUT THE AUTHOR

Heather Reyburn enjoyed an idyllic childhood in beautiful New Zealand, before settling on the Darling Downs in Queensland. With a passion for nature, animals, reading and all things farm related, it wasn't long before her rural lifestyle inspired dreams of writing stories of her own. She loves happy endings, history, suspense, and characters who remain with the reader long after "The End". When not writing, Heather is often found in the garden or spending time with her family.